KATE WINFIELD

ON THE OREGON TRAIL

In Jesus' Love,

Peter Marshall

Feb. '10

KATE WINFIELD

ON THE OREGON TRAIL

PETER MARSHALL
AND ANNA FISHEL

B&H
PUBLISHING GROUP

Nashville, Tennessee

978-0-8054-4397-4

Published by B&H Publishing Group,
Nashville, Tennessee

Dewey Decimal Classification: F
Subject Heading: OREGON NATIONAL HISTORIC TRAIL—
FICTION \ ADVENTURE FICTION

This book is a work of fiction, intended to entertain and inspire. Although it is based on actual historical events, some of the names, characters, places, and incidents are the products of the authors' imagination. In some cases, fictitious words or actions have been attributed to real individuals; these, too, are imagined.

1 2 3 4 5 6 7 8 • 12 11 10 09 08

DEDICATION

To the more than three hundred thousand courageous pioneer men, women, and children who braved the disease and death, perilous river crossings, blistering heat, horrific storms, choking alkali dust, freezing nights, and Indian attacks on the Oregon Trail. Conquering their fears, discouragements, and losses, they persevered and fulfilled the American dream of a nation that stretches from sea to shining sea.

ACKNOWLEDGMENTS

For her gracious and helpful research assistance, the authors are grateful to Sarah Le Compte, the director of the exquisitely well done Oregon Trail Interpretive Center in Baker City, Oregon.

THE CHARACTERS

THE WINFIELD FAMILY

Kate Winfield: Slim, auburn-haired Kate is seventeen in 1843, when her family embarks on the Oregon Emigrating Company's two thousand-mile trek from Independence, Missouri, to the Oregon Territory.

Jacob Winfield: Kate's father has struggled as a farmer in Missouri, but he sees this journey as his opportunity to start farming afresh in the fertile soil of Oregon.

Abigail Winfield: Kate's mother has reluctantly accepted her husband's decision to start a new life in Oregon, but leaving home and friends has torn her heart.

Jake Winfield: Kate's ten-year-old brother is setting forth on the greatest adventure of his young life, and his antics never fail to bring a smile to Kate's lips.

Old Joe: The Winfields' faithful hired hand, who, when he has been "thinkin' on things" with his "wisdom stick" brings forth godly words of counsel.

ON THE WAGON TRAIN

Arkansas: The crusty old mountain man and fur trapper is wise in the ways of the wilderness and the Indians.

Dr. Marcus Whitman: Medical doctor and missionary to the Cayuse Indians, he is returning home to his wife and mission station in Walla Walla, Oregon Territory.

John Prentiss: A handsome, green-eyed Philadelphian with whom Kate develops a deepening friendship.

John Gantt: Pilot for the wagon train, he has been hired by the Oregon Emigrating Company to guide them as far as Fort Hall.

ANIMALS

Scout: The black and tan dog's life is saved by Kate's father, and he soon becomes her constant companion and friend.

The Winfield oxen: Joshua, Caleb, Prudence, Patience, Balak, Balaam, Hannah, and Eli make it possible for the family to travel the Oregon Trail.

Midnight: The Winfields' coal-black draft horse.

Tess: The Winfields' milk cow.

1

THE WHIPPING

Wednesday, May 17

The black leather whip snaked through the air and snapped at the dog's right hindquarters. The animal yelped and collapsed into the dirt, a red welt opening up on its thin flank.

"Chase my cattle, will ya? I'll teach ya, ya dirty stray," the man hollered in a raspy voice, as he quickly coiled the whip for another strike.

Struggling slowly to his feet, the black and tan dog began to move away, but the whip once again hissed through the air and wrapped around his right hind leg. As the dog was jerked off his feet, the dust flew from his fur, and he went down again. This time, when he tried to stand his hindquarters wouldn't support him. He was hurt—badly.

Scattered across the dirt road and into the fields, the grimy cattle owner's cows roamed this way and that, mooing and bellowing loudly. A covered wagon, its pots and pans banging against the wagon bed, bounced along behind, driven by a scruffy-looking man barking orders at a team of four mules.

In the distance the waters of the Missouri River meandered through the fields like a long strand of gray yarn. Nearby the river port of Independence, Missouri, was teeming with activity. It was the jumping off point for those heading out on the trail to California or Oregon. Filled with harness and blacksmith shops, gunsmiths, wheelwrights, and even old trappers, the town was the perfect place to outfit a rig and get almost anything an emigrant might need.

Jacob Winfield had left his tall and slender young daughter, Kate, to guard their own small herd of cattle while he went into town to buy two oxen. With everyone busy around her, no one seemed to notice what was happening to this stray dog.

No one except Kate.

Suddenly, out of the corner of her eye, Kate spotted her father. Two new oxen the color of bread crust snorted and shook their big heads as they lumbered beside him in the noonday sun.

"Papa!" she yelled. "Papa!" Kate whipped her cloth bonnet off her auburn ponytail and frantically waved it in the air to get his attention.

At first Jacob didn't notice his daughter. His mind was on the task at hand. "Keep movin'!" he announced to the oxen. "I'm a mite thirsty myself." Her father flipped off his floppy hat and wiped his sweaty brow with a sleeve.

"Papa!" Kate yelled again, even louder this time.

At that moment Ole Joe's deep Virginia drawl sounded above the din as he tilted his head in her direction. "Mistah Jacob, I believe Miz Kate is tryin' to git yer attention." The black man stopped and pointed toward Kate.

"Papa! Help!" Kate cried, as she ran toward her father.

Jacob handed his riding crop to Joe.

"Papa, the man's whipping that dog!" Kate explained, grabbing his arm and pulling him toward the wounded animal.

Jacob Winfield was not a large man, but he had a kind heart and loved animals—even a stray dog with matted hair and a scrawny tail. He would do something about this. Kate was certain of that.

The dog had not moved under the cattle driver's threatening shadow. Terror filled its pleading black eyes as it looked at the whip in the man's hands. Kate could hear it whimpering over the distant sounds of hammering and banging.

"I'll give you $2.50 for the dog." Jacob scowled at the man as he reached into his shirt pocket for the coin. It glistened in his hand.

"You're as big a fool as this here mongrel," the man laughed. "You can have that good-fer-nothin' stray." He spat a stream of brown tobacco juice into the dirt, grabbed the Quarter Eagle from Jacob, and mounted his horse. "Good riddance," he sneered, as he rode off.

"I guess you've got yourself a dog, Kate," Papa smiled. "Let's get him back to our wagon." With that, Jacob scooped the hurt animal into his strong arms. The black and tan dog didn't flinch, even though blood now oozed from its wounds, and its right leg, once a walnut color, dangled in the air as her father lifted him.

When Kate reached over to stroke the dog's head, he licked her hand, grateful that someone cared.

2

SCOUT

Wednesday, May 17

A short while later, they arrived at their "home on wheels," as Kate's mother called it, a large family wagon and a smaller supply wagon. Papa and Ole Joe had fashioned the two wagon beds out of hickory wood back on their Livingston County farm in northwest Missouri. Papa had chosen hickory because he said it would resist shrinking in the dry air of the plains and the deserts they had to cross. The wagons had to be strong enough to carry their belongings the whole two thousand miles but light enough that their draft animals—oxen—could still pull them when loaded.

Kate knew that her father had learned from Hasting's *Emigrant's Guide to Oregon and California* that oxen were better for pulling wagons than mules for two reasons: one, mules were more expensive, nearly $100 each; and two, they were generally more stubborn. Papa had brought six oxen from home but had decided that he needed two more. He had bought them in Independence this morning and was bringing them back to camp when Kate had yelled for his help.

The larger wagon's bed was small—only four feet wide, ten feet long, and three feet deep. Its side boards were slanted out to keep rain from coming in under the edges of the bonnet Kate and her mother had made. Bows of bent hickory wood supported the homespun cotton fabric top, now gleaming white in the western sun, and provided only about six feet of head-room down the middle of the wagon. Kate's mother had sewn flaps on the front and puckering strings along the back for ventilation, privacy, and to keep out the dust. Papa told Kate that the two smaller front wheels would help the wagon turn more easily, and he forged tires of iron to protect all of the wheel rims. With its axles, tongue, and front seat, the wagon weighed about 1,300 pounds empty.

But, like all the other wagons waiting at the various camps around Independence, their wagon was far from empty. Inside were all the things Kate and her mother had packed not only for the trip but for the time when they finally arrived in the Willamette Valley of the Oregon Territory.

Abigail Winfield's head of long wavy coal black hair appeared out of the back of the wagon. Kate's mother hopped down, holding the folds of her long calico skirt and clutching a piece of paper in her right hand. Her light frame hardly made the wagon move. She put back on her head the blue bonnet that had slipped down her back.

"Jacob," she hollered as Joshua, their oldest ox, bellowed to nobody in particular. "There's a meeting down at Fitzhugh's Mill tomorrow for everyone who's leaving. A man dropped this here flyer off this morning."

Jacob laid the wounded dog down in the grass beside the front wheel. "Joe, take the new ones over there to graze with the others. I'll be there in a minute."

Kate could see the love in her Papa's eyes for her Mama. It was always there, even when he was exhausted. "I'll be going for sure, Abby," he replied as he brushed black dog hair off his sleeves and unlashed the buckle of the leather strap holding their wagon's repair box, called a jockey box.

"What's this?" Abby asked, a decided twinkle in her chocolate brown eyes.

"I was watching the herd, Mama, and I saw a man beating this dog with a whip. Papa came along just in time." Kate undid the ribbon around her long ponytail, tugged her auburn hair back with her hands, and retied it with the ribbon. "I just couldn't let him do it, Mama."

Kate always took care of living things. One time Papa had brought her a sick cat that had mysteriously appeared in the loft of their barn, and Kate nursed it back to health. Another time it was a rabbit. This time, it was going to be a dog.

"Looks like we got ourselves another patient," Abby replied. "Fetch that bucket of water right there, Kate, and I'll grab some bandages from our medical bag. Let's see if we can't clean him up.

"Kate, Mrs. Stewart is pregnant. Her baby is due in early July. Maybe we can help," she added, as she washed the blood and dirt off the dog's flanks and hind leg.

"I would like that, Mama," Kate responded, stroking the head of her new pet to keep him still.

"You found a dog?" Kate's younger brother could hardly contain his excitement as he dashed up and slid into the side of the wagon. Another boy was with him.

"Jake, watch out," Abby scolded as she dabbed at the dog's wounds. "You'll loosen one of them boards doing stunts like that."

With jet-black hair and turquoise eyes, Jacob Ashton Winfield III looked every bit like a Winfield, the "spittin' image" Papa would always say, which really meant he looked just like Papa. Kate's little brother was ten and often a bother, but he could get Kate to smile faster than anyone.

"Sorry, Mama," Jake replied, catching his breath. "Papa, you know I been wanting a dog a long time."

The wooden box cover slammed after Papa finally retrieved his iron hammer. "Talk to yer sister, Jake," Papa replied, heading out toward the supply wagon and Ole Joe, who had just tethered the two new oxen to some stakes in the ground. "This one's hers."

With a slight look of dejection, Jake quickly rallied. "Oh, I almost forgot. Mama, this here's my new friend, Elisha. His camp's right over there." He pointed toward two wagons under large poplar trees. "He has a twin named Warren. Looks jest like him, too!"

"Nice to meet you, Elisha," Abby offered. "Aren't you an Applegate?"

Elisha pulled his straw hat off his head, revealing a tussle of blond hair. "Yes 'm," he replied. "My Papa's name is Lindsey and my Mama's Betsy."

Just then Jake broke in. "Can we go play now? I stuck all the firewood for lunch over there." He pointed toward a haphazard pile of sticks.

"For now," Abby replied as she ripped some strips off a piece of coarse cotton tow cloth. "But stay within hollerin' distance. I'll be needin' you to fetch some water when we finish mending this dog.

"Kate, I think his leg is broken," her mother murmured with a frown. "But this splint ought to hold it straight until it heals," she said, winding cloth strips around two stout sticks that she had placed on either side of the dog's right hind leg.

"I think I'll call him Scout, Mama." The dog's tongue felt wet and rough as it licked the top of Kate's slender fingers. Scout liked her, and Kate felt sure that he was going to be a good companion. It must have been God's hand that brought them together, she thought with a smile, because if she hadn't found him when she did the man would have killed him.

Kate was hoping that this whole trip was in God's hands. Papa certainly thought so. "The Lord is about to expand our horizons," was the way he put it.

At that moment in the spring of 1843, little did seventeen-year-old
Catherine Jessica Winfield suspect how much her horizons were about to be
stretched, and how hard her faith would be tested.

3

"WE'S LEAVIN' THE UNITED STATES, MISSY!"

Sunday, May 21

They got roads, Kate?" Jake gobbled down a last bite of soda biscuit and strawberry jam. "Two thousand miles is an awful long way to go without roads."

Tin plates clinking and people talking in the nearby camps, coupled with roosters crowing and distant mooing, formed a backdrop to breakfast today. Kate could also hear the "hoo-hoo-too-hoo" of owls conversing somewhere in the distance.

"Papa said that at first we'll be following the rivers along the same trails the Santa Fe traders use, Jake." In the still crisp morning light, Kate rinsed off their breakfast plates. "We'll go along the Platte River Valley, through the Great Desert, and then later across two mountain ranges, the Blues and the Cascades."

"What if there aren't any roads?" Jake exclaimed.

"We'll have to trust our pilot, Jake," Papa responded patiently. "John Gantt knows the way. He's been as far as Fort Hall."

Papa was adjusting the long leather straps on their team of six oxen, already yoked and hitched with chains to the larger wagon. Getting the oxen ready had been hard work for him and Joe, and Papa already looked as if he had been at it all day. His nutmeg muslin shirt was stained with sweat and Joe's didn't look any better. Papa didn't swear very much, but he had come pretty close this morning. "Yoking these blame oxen together could send a man to hell, Joe, just for his words," Kate had heard him mutter when the oxen refused to cooperate.

Papa had placed the two new oxen, now the biggest and the youngest, in the lead, but they didn't seem very happy about it. On their part, the other yoked pairs—Prudence and Patience, and Joshua and Caleb—didn't seem happy about being teamed with the new oxen, either. The new ones didn't have names yet, because Papa said he needed to get to know them first. "Listen here, boys," he declared, as they tossed their heads and snorted. "You and your cousin got a ways to go today as a pair, so you'd best put your minds to it."

Kate placed their tin plates inside a wide pocket sewn into the wagon's bonnet, one of many such pockets.

Scout was lying on a blanket and thumped his tail softly when Kate petted him.

"Scout, you've got to stay put now until that leg gets better," Kate ordered as she rubbed the scruff of his neck. "I'm going to get you well, so you can run like the wind. But, no jumping out of the wagon now, you hear me?" Scout's walnut colored ears perked up as he stretched out on the blanket, his broken hind leg sticking straight out. He seemed to have recovered some from the savage whipping, but he wasn't going to be doing any running for a while and he knew it.

"The meeting this morning went well, Abby." Jacob yanked a dirty red kerchief out of his back pocket to mop the grime off his neck. "We met with Dr. Whitman, who runs a mission in Walla Walla. He strongly believes this number of wagons can make it all the way across the mountains. We're organizing ourselves as a company, because we need some sort of order once we get away from civilization into Indian Territory. We're calling it the Oregon Emigrating Company."

"Indian Territory?" Jake perked up as he handed Kate his tin breakfast plate to be rinsed off.

"Now, Mistah Jake," Joe added, scratching his short wooly white hair. "I hear them Indians ain't goin' to hurt us none. They don't seem to mind folks who is just passin' through."

"How 'bout tying Tess to the back of the wagon?" he added, as he fastened the horseshoe pins of Hannah and Eli's yoke snugly around their necks, readying them to pull the supply wagon.

"I hear Indians scalp people, Joe, and cut them in pieces," Jake persisted, untying a long rope from a poplar branch and escorting their milk cow toward the back of the smaller wagon. "Elisha told me so."

Ole Joe grinned widely. "If that's the case, young 'un, then we'll have to do a heap of prayin' to the Almighty, won't we?"

Kate gave Scout one last pat and waved a forefinger at him as an admonishment to stay put before jumping off the backboard that supported her Mama's precious rocker and her Papa's farm plow. The air caught her lavender linen skirt, showing her new black cowhide boots, which she had soaked and broken in so they would be ready for the trip—a trip that meant walking. The wagons had no room, and besides, riding in them over the rough terrain was horrible. So, all of the Winfields would be walking.

"How many people are going, Papa?" she asked.

"We've got more than six hundred people in the Company right now, Kate," Jacob replied. "But that can change because people will come and go."

"What about officers, Jacob?" Abby's question revealed her attempt to show interest in the workings of the wagon train.

"Burnett said we needed to get to know one another first. The Company decided to wait on the voting until we reach the Kansas River," he finished.

Kate's mother hadn't wanted to leave their home. She had accepted her husband's decision, as any good wife would do, but Kate sensed that she was only going because he said they had to. One time she had clutched a linen tablecloth to her chest so long that Kate thought she'd never let it go. Another time Kate discovered her dabbing her eyes while boxing up their few pieces of china. Sometimes Mama would take in a deep breath before tackling a task, as if the work required extra effort. Kate thought that today Mama was putting forth extra effort to care about the trip.

Within the hour the great caravan of covered wagons began to move out across the green meadows toward Elm Grove, the rendezvous point thirty-five miles west of Independence and beyond the Missouri state line. As the wagons ahead of them rumbled forward, Jacob laid the riding crop on the Winfield oxen, and their two wagons shifted into motion. Abby, Kate, and Jake walked alongside the larger wagon, while Joe guided Hannah and Eli as they pulled the smaller wagon, piled high with supplies tied under a thick canvas cover. Behind the wagon, Tess and their packhorse, a black Irish draft horse named Midnight, plodded along through spring grasses that hundreds of hooves were quickly treading into a road. Bringing up the rear and creating a large dust cloud was the wagon train's herd of cattle, urged forward by the mounted drivers appointed for the day.

The family had only gone about five hundred yards, however, when the two lead oxen suddenly grunted in the morning air and abruptly stopped.

"Git up there, boys," Jacob ordered, his voice loud and clear. "Get movin'. You can't stay here." Papa flicked his riding crop on their hindquarters, but it didn't do any good. Saliva dripped from their mouths as the two bovine leaned their big brown heads away from one another and tugged against their yoke. They weren't moving.

"Maybe the wagon's too heavy, Jacob," Abby volunteered. "After all, we're toting eight hundred pounds of flour and five hundred pounds of bacon, not to mention our trunk and other things."

"I've got six of them, Abby," Jacob replied in his let-me-take-care-of-this voice. "They're just being lazy."

With that, Jacob scooped up a handful of rocks from a rut and began pelting the beasts on their rear ends. "Get moving!" he yelled. "What's the matter with you?" Her Papa hollered so loud that Kate saw brown larks fly out of the trees across the meadow.

The oxen started to move again, but after two more of these stops, Kate could see the veins bulging in Papa's neck.

Just then a man in a floppy hat and oat colored pants cantered up on a large roan quarter horse. The man held a nasty looking bullwhip in one hand.

"You look like you might be needin' some help, Jacob," the man said as he reined in his horse.

"They keep stopping, Lindsey," Jacob replied, clearly exasperated.

"Sometimes these animals can be as ornery as mules." Applegate's whip had a stiff handle and long tapered leather braids. "Once they learn, though, they'll be just fine."

The man jerked his wrist sharply. The long tip of his whip made a loud cracking sound in the air as it whizzed past both lead animals. The snap was so precise Kate was sure it could have flicked a gnat off an ox's rump if Mr. Applegate had wanted it to. His whip never touched either animal, but it did jolt them out of their reverie. The two lead oxen pushed against their yokes and began to plod through the short-bladed grass.

"Which ones are the new ones?" Applegate asked.

"These two," Jacob replied, pointing to the leaders.

"Might need to put them in the middle for awhile, until they learn. In time they'll probably become your best pair." With that, he reined his horse to the left and cantered off across the field ahead of them.

At Jacob's nod Joe unhitched Prudence and Patience and put them in the front of the team. "Maybe we should name these two Balaam and Balak," Joe offered as he fastened the new oxen into the middle position.

"They're as ornery as those fellows in the Bible, that's for sure," Jacob chuckled. And the names stuck.

By the time the sun reached its zenith in an azure blue sky a few hours later, both Kate's black boots and her long lavender skirt were coated with yellow trail dust. A cloud of gnats seemed to follow her every step, swarming around her head. Well, she thought, at least I can clean up when we stop tonight.

Joe's low voice interrupted her thought. "See that cabin over there, Miz Kate?"

"What cabin, Joe?" They were walking through clouds of dandelion spores.

"Over there."

"Are you thinking on it, Joe?" Kate asked in a lighthearted tone. Their old hired hand liked to "think on" things every once in awhile, mostly when he was "sittin' and thinkin'" by himself. Jake would sometimes sneak up on him and try to scare him for fun, but Joe always seemed to know Jake was there, and he never seemed to mind at all.

"Might be needin' to think on this," Joe replied with a smile.

Far to their right, a thin column of blue-gray smoke curled up from the stone chimney of a tiny cabin. Large elm and cottonwood logs had been chinked together with mud using dovetailed notches at each corner. On a narrow front porch, two empty cane-back chairs waited for their owners to "sit a' rockin'" in the warmth of a summer's eve. Behind the cabin, cattle grazed contentedly, and in front scrawny chickens pecked at the ground.

"That there's the end of civilization for awhile, Miz Kate," Joe said, scrunching his floppy straw hat against his chest in reverence, the hat his deceased wife Bessie had given him years ago.

"What do you mean, Joe?" Kate asked, letting her skirt go for a minute.

"We's leavin' the United States, Missy, and that's a fact."

As the circles of smoke disappeared behind them in the distance, Kate found herself taking very deliberate steps. Without so much as a word, they had bid farewell to the state of Missouri and had entered the wilderness.

The United States was now behind them.

4

A NEW LIFE DAWNS

Monday, May 22

The sliver of the last quarter moon in May hung in the dark sky. Kate could feel Scout's moist breath at her cheek. She resisted opening her eyes until the thumping of his scratching for fleas with his good hind leg thoroughly awakened her. There was no sound from her parents' tent. Kate rolled onto her stomach on top of her soft bedroll, squared her nightcap, and settled her chin into the palms of her hands.

"It's going to be a clear day, boy." She whispered the words so as not to wake up her brother before the 4 a.m. bugle. As she breathed in the fresh morning air and listened to the first chirps of a lark, she thought about home and all the things they had done to get this far.

Getting the free acres was what drew Papa to the Oregon Territory— that, and getting them out of their "money hole," as he called it. Kate knew Papa had read Hastings' *Guide* so often the pages were frayed. He had already moved them once before, all the way from Virginia when Kate was eight, and now he was pulling up their family's roots again. "This time, I'll do better as a farmer," he had said. Mama's response had been emphatic. "Jacob, this time it *has* to work."

Once Papa had made the decision to leave, he had easily sold the farm and heavy equipment to a man who had just arrived with his family from Pennsylvania. The $1,500 Papa had been paid was a fair price, and he had used $1,000 of it to help them get outfitted for the trip. That was a lot of money to Kate's family, but Papa believed it would be worth it.

The man organizing this particular wagon train, Peter Burnett, also believed the long and difficult journey would be worth all the effort. In fact, he was determined that this train would be the first one to take wagons all the way to Oregon. Papa trusted that Burnett knew what he was doing, and that was good enough for Kate.

Her and her mother's questions about what to bring had been endless. How much should they pack? What food should they take? What cooking utensils would they need? How much clothing should they carry? What herbs and medical supplies would be right?

Papa's questions had been different. How much farm equipment should he sell off? How much should he take? How could he build a sturdy enough wagon, one that could float across rivers? What animals should they take? What tools were necessary, not only for the trip but also for their new farm in Oregon?

As Scout sighed in her ear, Kate thought of the most important question her farming father had faced: what seeds should they take? They had finally chosen wheat and barley seed, corn and peas, pumpkin and squash, the basic crops they needed for starting over. Even brown flax seeds to grow the yarn to make their clothing. It was all there in the hollow dried shell of a large gourd, securely tied inside the wagon's bonnet.

In Missouri, the Winfields and their neighbors had used gourds, which were hard-skinned relatives of pumpkins and squash, for all kinds of things. Jake had grown one to store crickets last summer, and Mama had made some for her tinctures.

This particular gourd was shaped like a bottle. After months of drying it out, Kate had painted it with blue and green leather dye. Now, its mouth plugged by a corncob, the gourd carried their precious seeds.

She and Mama had worked day and night through the winter getting ready for the trip—cooking and canning, sewing and packing. They had preserved eggs and pickled beef. They had dried herbs and mixed special medicines. They had sewn clothes and chosen special pieces of Grandma Foster's china. They had painted the cotton material for the wagon's bonnet with water-repellent linseed oil. They had carefully packed the big trunk and placed it in the wagon. Papa said they could only take four pieces of furniture, and they finally decided on Grandpa Winfield's walnut plantation desk, Grandma Foster's bentwood rocking chair, and two straight-back chairs.

Even then, Mama wasn't sure they had made all the right decisions. They had never done anything like this. Mama's way of handling her doubts was to put it in God's hands. "We'll do the best we can and trust the Lord to take care of it," she said.

The actual leaving was the hardest. Close friends had walked with them for the first few miles alongside the wagons, but finally they stopped. Kate and her mother had both cried as every westward step of the oxen made their friends grow smaller and smaller in the distance, their tearful goodbyes lingering in the morning air.

Just then Kate's thoughts were interrupted by the loud notes of a bugle echoing through the camp. It was the morning call, answered by a friendly Bantam rooster. Even before the sun had risen Kate could feel the excitement in the air.

Three hours later the clamor of hundreds of emigrants could be heard across the wide-open fields. "Hee, girl, this way. Haw! Over here!" The men shouted to get their teams plodding forward. New iron-rimmed wheels with elm hubs and ash spokes creaked as they got under way. Tin pots and pans clanked against the sides of 120 wagons. Tar buckets and butter churns swung and banged in rhythmic motion. Chickens in cages squawked every time their wagons bumped over rocks. Children with bare feet hollered in glee, scampering ahead only to be called back by concerned mothers. More than five thousand head of cattle, many of them mooing, added a resonant chorus to the whole scene. Fifty of those cattle belonged to Kate's father.

Swaying back and forth, each wagon rolled through the yellow sunflowers and tall green prairie grasses, beside and behind scores of other wagons, some painted in bright greens or pale blues, others with stained wood. The morning sunlight transformed the newly-sewn white wagon bonnets into a magical moving landscape. As the wagons lurched forward, the crescendo of noises escalated. They were on their way to Oregon—and a whole new life!

5

ARKANSAS

Monday, May 22

Even at noon, excitement still permeated the air. Kate could hear the cries of "whoa" as the lead wagons in the column began to pull into groups on the prairie grass. It was time for the "nooning," an hour or so of lunch and rest for both the herd and the emigrants.

"Gantt says to stop here, folks. It's as good a place as any." In one single motion, the rider slid out of his stirrups and off the saddle on his dark brown and white spotted Appaloosa, as if he had done it thousands of times before. Kate noticed the rifle resting in a holster tied near the saddle horn and the red blanket rolled up behind.

"Name's Cutler, folks. Arkansas Cutler." He tugged off his furry beaver cap, its tail swinging in the wind, revealing a ruddy brow weathered from years in the sun. "But you can call me Saw."

The man's tattered gray beard vibrated with his bottom lip when he talked. Kate tried not to smile and quickly eyed Jake to see how he was responding to this odd character.

"Nice to meet you, ladies," he bowed. "You, too, gents," he nodded.

Kate had heard about mountain men before, but she had never actually met one. The man's bushy gray hair dangled to his shoulders, covering up any hint of ears. He wore a midnight blue plaid flannel shirt, and his waist was encircled with a broad belt of leather holding a Bowie knife and a pistol. Deerskin breeches decorated with porcupine quills and thick long fringes down both seams revealed many years among the Indians. Tiny colorful beads lined the edges on his moccasins.

"Glad to meet you, Arkansas." Jacob held out his hand.

Arkansas shook Papa's hand with vigor and then stepped toward Ole Joe, who had just tied Midnight and Tess near some clumps of flowering

15

Indian grass. "Glad to make your acquaintance, too," the mountaineer offered.

"Won't you have a cup of this morning's coffee?" Abby asked.

"Be much obliged, Ma'am. Been thirsty for it." With that, Arkansas plunked down on the ground. "What's yer name, young lady?" he asked.

"Kate, sir," Kate replied. She had a firm grip on the rope around Scout's neck, whose furiously wagging tail indicated that the bandaged dog would have jumped all over the trapper if he could have. "And this is my brother, Jake."

Jake couldn't resist. "Are you a real mountain man? I mean a trapper?" His turquoise eyes widened like saucers.

"That I am, boy." Arkansas chuckled through yellowed teeth.

Jake snatched a ham biscuit sandwich from the straw basket Abby had positioned on a stump.

"Where you from, Arkansas?" Abby pulled out their morning coffee pot and poured their visitor a cup.

"Everywhere, I guess, Ma'am," he replied. "Been trappin' since '34. Part of the Rocky Mountain Fur Company with Bridger and Carson fer awhile. Took off on my own a few years back when the beaver pelt trade began dryin' up thanks to that thar French king, Louis-Philippe. Them Europeans ain't likin' beaver hats anymore; it's silk now. So I got myself into takin' folks like you cross country."

"You been far, Saw?" Jacob was unhitching Balak from the long iron pin that ran vertically through the yoke's middle and attached him and Balaam to their chain. While they wouldn't be free from the yoke itself, the animals could graze together easily with the other oxen and rest before their afternoon journey.

"Been all the way to the Pacific more 'n once." Arkansas gulped down the liquid in two quick swallows. "But never with a wagon train. This is a first." With that, he jumped up and started to leave as fast as he had come. "Thanks fer the hospitality, folks. Best git m'self goin'. It's my job to find us a place to camp tonight."

A short while later, the Winfields had just finished eating when Jane Mills arrived from her family's wagon, parked right behind theirs. She was a slender girl with curly blonde ringlets sneaking out from a quilted bonnet. The blue in her bonnet and matching blouse brought out the striking blue color of her big round eyes.

"Mrs. Winfield, can Kate come with me to find Father?" Jane asked. "He's visiting Mr. Applegate. We won't be gone long."

With a nod from Mama, Kate and Jane were off.

"I'm not quite sure where the Applegates' wagon is, Kate. Do you know?" Jane tried to avoid a small swarm of bees buzzing through some clover.

"They all look alike to me." Kate cringed and followed her friend. Bees were not her favorite insect. "But we'll find them."

The girls weaved in and out among the wagons. A mother was singing her baby into a nap with a lullaby. Two men were munching on dried beef and discussing a missing horse. Joel Hembree, a six-year-old boy, and a little girl dressed in a red pinafore played hide 'n seek around their covered wagon.

"I think that's them," Jane announced at last when five wagons bound together by a group of milling men, women, and children came into sight.

At just that moment, a booming male voice surged over the top of two wagons to Kate's right.

"Here's to the buffalo you're going to kill, Lancefield," the voice announced for the world to hear.

"And here's to your new business venture, Atkins, whatever it may be," another replied, just as loudly.

Kate slowed down. The empty space between the two wagons gave her a full view. Three men were sipping a bubbly liquid in clear tall stemmed glasses. A long-necked champagne bottle had been placed on top of a linen-covered barrel. The glasses chinked together as the men toasted one another.

Each man was dressed in fine breeches, matching ascots, and dark waist-coats, as if he were going to the city instead of heading out on the prairie. The bright red hair of one of the men peeked out from under a tall silk hat.

"Who are *they*?" Kate asked Jane.

"They're from back east, Father says," Jane explained under her breath. "That one with the red hair is Lancefield Johnson. He and Mr. Atkins, the one pouring another glass, are from Boston. That other one, Douglas some-thing, is from Philadelphia."

"They must think clothes make the man," Kate quipped as she hiked up her linen skirt to step around a clump of flowering bluestems.

"They're greenhorns, to be sure," Jane retorted.

Just then Kate noticed a fourth gentleman at the backside of the second wagon. He was combing the white mane of a dark gold Palomino. This man didn't look as old as the others. His dark wavy hair fell softly to his neck, and his red plaid shirt seemed a bit big on his thin frame. The man had spotted Kate and was close enough to have heard what the girls were discussing. With a slight grin, he caught Kate's eye as she walked by and winked at her.

"Ma'am," he nodded.

Kate felt her face flush, as she sucked in a deep breath and quickly accelerated her pace to catch up with Jane.

She had to wonder, though. Were these men the kind that a young woman had to watch out for on the trail?

6

STIRRING UP TROUBLE

Wednesday, May 24

Over the next few days, travel on the prairie settled into a comfortable routine. Each morning began at 4 a.m. when the wake-up bugle sounded. The last shift of men guarding the enormous herd of cattle would soon be joined by other men, and together they would round up strays and gather the herd into a circle by 5 a.m. Husbands would check on their cattle and hitch up their ox teams while the wives fixed breakfast.

By 7 a.m. the families would have loaded everything back on the wagons. Sharp on the stroke of the hour, the bugle would sound again, and the wagons would begin rolling out. Sometimes they traveled in a double column, and sometimes there were many columns stretched out across the wide-open grassy prairie, depending on how bad the dust was. At times wagons would compete for a position in front, which Kate soon discovered was an attempt to avoid the dust being thrown up by those in the lead. Before the daylight faded from the western sky, the wagons would camp for the night, forming various circles or corrals.

On Wednesday night the Winfields' wagon jostled into a place behind the Applegates in a corral of about forty wagons. Jacob and Joe guided their teams along the line of the large circle laid out by John Gantt. Each driver stopped his team just behind the wagon in front, so that his wagon tongue almost touched it. This way, all the wagons in their group formed a corral. The oxen and horses could graze within the circle but weren't able to wander off.

As Jacob and Joe were unpinning the U-shaped hickory bows around Balaam and Balaak's necks, Lindsey Applegate approached them. After greeting Kate and Abby, who were lugging a sack of cornmeal from the supply wagon, he turned toward Jacob.

"Just want to warn you, Jacob. That Englishman, Miles Eyers, is stirring up trouble." The headband around Applegate's floppy brown hat was as dark with sweat as was his navy bib shirt.

He went on, "Eyers doesn't have cattle and is telling folks he's sick of waiting around for those of us who do."

Jacob heaved the heavy yoke onto the ground. "We're almost to the Kansas River, Lindsey," he replied as he began unfastening the yoke on Patience and Prudence. "Looks like we're already needing officers to sort out the problems."

Applegate's fingers combed through his sandy hair before he plopped his hat back on his head. "How are your new oxen working, anyway?"

"Just fine, thanks to a little prodding from a friend." Jacob smiled.

Not thirty minutes later, the sound of a braying mule caught Kate's attention. Water sloshed out of the wooden bucket as she set it down near Scout, who was tied to one of the supply wagon's front wheels.

"Winfield!" The word was harsh to Kate's ears as she whirled around. "Winfield!"

Riding like a king on his donkey, the man had long gray sideburns that traveled halfway down his jaw. His belly protruded over his belt and he was jabbing the pudgy forefinger of his right hand straight up in the air. "I'm needing to talk to you, Winfield."

The flap on the tent Jacob had just erected opened. Jacob emerged, brushing the dirt off his palms.

"What can I do for you, Mr. Eyers?" Jacob asked. Kate detected caution in her Papa's voice.

Eyers squinted his beady eyes as if the sun was at high noon. A large scowl etched even more wrinkles in the folds of his face. "I'm one to face facts with facts," the man snarled, his tone clearly offensive. "We got a problem, and it's your cattle. They're slowing us up, and I'm not going to guard them when I don't own any."

Just then the tip of an old stick emerged through the flaps of Joe's tent followed by Joe himself, holding a corncob pipe. Kate recognized the stick, a precious possession of Joe's since before she was born. He called it his wisdom stick. "Long as I got this stick, Miz Kate," Joe would say. "I knows what to do." Kate figured Joe was about to take a walk with his stick and his pipe, and "think on things," as he put it.

Eyers caught sight of Ole Joe. "I heard you had a nigger with you, Winfield. What's he doing here? We don't need the likes of him where we're going."

Kate held her breath. Her Mama's family had owned Joe since he was a young boy and had given him and Bessie to Mama as a wedding gift. But Papa didn't believe in slavery, so when they moved to Missouri, Papa offered the couple their freedom. Joe and Bessie had stayed on as hired hands, both of them as beloved as ever. Kate knew that Joe had been saving his wages and that he was planning to buy his own little "piece of God's earth" in Oregon. What would Papa say to Eyers?

Every muscle in Jacob's face tightened as he squared his broad shoulders and pursed his lips. "Eyers—" he spoke deliberately through clenched teeth. "Joe is my man and he is a part of our family. We do not use the word *nigger*, and I will thank you not to use it either." When Papa finished, his blue green eyes almost looked black as they glared at the man on the mule.

With that Eyers jerked his mule's head and trotted off. "We'll see about this cow issue," he hollered over his shoulder.

For a few seconds the tension from Eyers's visit hovered in the warm evening air. Then Papa spoke. "Joe," he said, a definite sadness in his tone. "I'm mighty sorry about that."

"Ain't no fault of yers, Mistah Jacob." Joe shook his head. "But I'm hopin' it won't git any worse as we go along."

Kate figured Joe would definitely be "thinkin' on things" tonight.

7

THE KANSAS RIVER

Friday–Tuesday, May 26–30

Soon the wagon train faced their first real challenge—crossing the Kansas River. From school Kate remembered that the river was a natural and easy means of transport for a tribe of Plains Indians known as the Caws, and for French fur trappers, and that it meandered from west to east for many miles before it eventually joined the Missouri River. In 1804 the Lewis and Clark expedition had camped there at the river's mouth. Now the wagons were traveling along the river's southern bank on their way to the Oregon Territory.

"The river's mighty swollen, Joe," Kate observed as she drank in the thick smell of the moist air and swatted away a fly. A lone white heron opened its yellow beak with a deep croak and took off in low flight from the far bank. "I guess it's the spring rains. Is Mr. Gantt sure there isn't any shallow place to ford?"

"That's what yer Papa said, Missy. From the looks of things, we'll be needin' to float 'em across." Joe frowned as he lifted one of their wagon wheels out of the water. He had been soaking it for a couple of hours, because it had shrunk away from its iron rim in the heat, and he was trying to get the wood to swell.

"How long will it take to get our wagons across?" Kate asked, balancing herself against a river birch and knocking the mud off her boots before they headed back to their wagons.

"A few days, I reckon. We gots lots of wagons." The creases in Joe's brow told Kate he was clearly worried. This was the first time they had ever crossed a river like this with wagons and cattle, and they were going to have to learn by doing it. Kate was thankful that everyone in her family, including Joe, knew how to swim, but the swimming hole back at the farm looked tame compared to this.

After returning to their campsite, Joe and Jacob worked on slipping the iron rim over the wooden wheel. In the meantime, Abby let Kate unwrap Scout's bandages. The wounds needed air now. The dog hobbled about in the grass, holding his still splinted leg out straight, barking playfully at Midnight and Tess. But their twitching tails indicated they weren't happy about his antics.

"Calm that dog, Kate," Jacob ordered over his shoulder. "I'll not have him bothering the animals."

A short while later, Abby and Kate had prepared a supper of beans and sowbelly for the family. Kate sprinkled some cheese over her plate and swatted at the ever-present gnats diving into her hair.

"Joe, we don't want the wagons to leak." Jacob's fork scraped against his tin plate. "We'll need to caulk them. You and I can take care of the big one. Abby, you and Kate can caulk the supply wagon." He swallowed a mouthful of beans.

"Seems like the independent spirit is getting the best of us, Abby," he continued. "Eyers and some of the other folks are itching to get across the river quick, so they've worked out a ferry arrangement with a Frenchman named Papin who lives near here. His rates are way too high for us. Tomorrow I'm going to help Burnett and the others build a ferry for the rest of us."

"Papa, how do you build a ferry?" The buttermilk in Jake's cup created a thick white mustache on his upper lip. He licked it off.

Jacob wiped his own mouth with the back of his hand. "It'll be a platform of poles, Jake, lashed together on top of two dugout canoes," he explained. "We'll roll each wagon onto the raft one at a time and then pull it across by long ropes attached to the ends."

"Sounds like a lot of work." Jake's shoulders slumped as if he were carrying a heavy weight. "I think I'd rather help with the caulkin'."

Caulking a wagon was a lot of work too—hot work, especially in late May on the prairie. The next day Joe heated some of their pine tar in an iron kettle over a blazing fire. Then Abby dropped tow cloth rags in the pot to soak up the tar. Next they poked long sticks into the kettle and lifted each rag out, one by one, being careful not to get even one drop of the blistering liquid on their skin. The blackened rags were stuffed in the cracks between the wagon boards and pounded down with a hammer or chisel. The last step was to smear even more scorching tar over the tops as a seal.

On the morning of the fourth day, it was the turn of the Winfields' watertight wagons to cross the river. The lapping of the waves against the muddy bank was quiet compared with the splashing and yelling from the river. Kate and Abby and Jake, who had planted themselves under a tree, were watching Papa and Joe lead their oxen into the water and across the channel. Caleb and Hannah bellowed loudly the whole way across, especially when they reached the middle and the water covered their backs.

"Are those Caw Indians over there, Mama?" Kate asked as she pulled her lavender flowered bonnet off her head in the shade. Kate knew that the Caw Indians lived on the Plains, but she had never seen one. Two men, more than six feet tall, wore colorful blankets draped around their shoulders. Their heads had been shaved, except for a tuft on the top, which had been dyed red and looked exactly like a rooster's crown. Kate couldn't take her eyes off them. They were different, that was sure, but they were quite regal, and Kate found herself growing interested in them.

"Some people call this the Caw River after them," Abby added, propping her elbows on her knees. "Arkansas says they're friendly, so we needn't worry."

Just then a man leading some cattle across the river yelled and then sank out of sight. "Mama!" Kate exclaimed. "That man's going to drown!" Her eyes were riveted on the drama unfolding in front of her.

Within seconds, two men who were in the river splashed over to help. The drowning man, frantic for air, had resurfaced. As the men reached him, he grabbed one of them by the throat, nearly choking him. Everyone on shore watched the drowning man struggle with his rescuers until one of them finally hit him squarely in the jaw and knocked him out. The two tired rescuers then dragged the man's limp body to the opposite shore. Kate wondered if Papa and Joe had even seen what happened, since it had happened behind them and they never turned around. Now they were leading their dripping oxen up onto the far bank.

"I guess that man'll be saying his prayers tonight, Mama, won't he," Jake surmised as he started digging another hole for his sand castle.

Mama's breath was long and slow before she replied. "Children, I think Mr. Vaughn has taught us an important lesson. Even people that know how to swim can drown."

Unfortunately a second hard lesson came immediately. Downriver the Frenchman's ferry was carrying the Zachary family's heavily loaded and uncovered wagon, including two daughters. To Kate's dismay, the raft suddenly capsized, catapulting the youngsters and all the belongings into the water. Just as quickly the two Caw Indians suddenly flung off their blankets and bounded into the water. With strong swift strokes, they quickly reached the two screaming girls and brought them safely back to the near shore. Everyone learned a lesson from this too: lighter loads are far less dangerous.

Almost before she knew what she was doing, however, Kate found herself scrambling through the weeds and mud along the river bank down toward the Zachary family. The Indians, dripping and huddled off to one side, were being ignored. Someone had to tell them, Kate thought. Someone had say "thanks" for saving the girls' lives, and Kate just knew that she was that person. Something—or someone—had prompted her to go.

With broad hand gestures, Kate tried to say "thank you" in sign language. Within moments a broad smile crossed the thin bronze lips of each brave. They nodded their heads, turned silently on their bare feet, and walked away. To the lapping of the waves and the sounds of emigrants still crossing the river, Kate watched them pad up the bank.

Later, as she lay on her bedroll, she found herself wondering what those Indians were really like and why people were afraid of them.

8

THE DOG DECREE

Thursday, June 1

After supper in the evening, the notes of "Turkey in the Straw" from Ole Joe's fiddle drew a large group of women and children, including Kate's friend Jane, to the Winfields' camp while the men attended the voting. Under a darkening sky, Ole Joe tapped his cowhide boots in the dirt and wagged his head in time with the melodies, while his chin rested on the fiddle. Now he switched to "Old Dan Tucker," a new and popular song:

> *Old Dan Tucker was a mighty man,*
> *He washed his face in a fryin' pan . . .*
> *Combed his head with a wagon wheel*
> *And he died with the toothache in his heel.*

Clapping her hands with the others, Kate watched Joe's fingers fly up and down the fingerboard. Usually the tune was familiar, but sometimes Joe would improvise, adding sharps and flats and his own distinct melody. Kate loved to hear Ole Joe play the fiddle, because he could make even the saddest heart happy—in spite of the fact that he couldn't read a note of music.

"You should have seen them run, Abby," Papa reported after he had returned from the election of the officers of the train. "Hundreds of men whooping and hollering, waving their hats and following their candidates."

Kate knew this was what everyone called "running for office." The candidates lined up, and at a signal started running across the fields. Those who wanted to vote for them would run after them in a single-file line, and the candidate with the greatest number of men behind him would win.

"Who won, Jacob?" Abby asked, her chair rocking silently on the ground while they all listened to Joe's fiddle. "Peter Burnett, by far," Papa replied, sitting down beside her. "Tomorrow night we'll divide the company into divisions and elect subcaptains, just like a military unit. It'll help keep order."

Just then Edward Stevenson and William Vaughn, the man who had almost drowned, strode up to their campsite.

"We're not going to let anyone shoot our dogs!" Stevenson declared, gripping the barrel of his rifle. "I got me two mastiffs and Vaughn here is traveling with a dog. Are you with us, Jacob?"

The music of Joe's fiddle abruptly ended in the middle of a tune. The circles of women abandoned their talking. Mama quit rocking. Kate broke off her conversation with Jane. Even the children grew quiet. For a moment it felt as if the entire world had stopped.

"Jacob, what's he talking about?" Abby broke the silence.

"The Dog Decree," Jacob sighed. "I wasn't going to tell you."

"Dog Decree?" Kate's voice and others echoed her mother's.

"Ladies, I'm afraid some people believe the dogs' howling and bark-ing will cause problems with the Indians. The Council voted to kill all the dogs."

"Are you with us or not?" Stevenson demanded.

Kate's jaw tightened. She couldn't believe her ears. Surely this wasn't happening. How could anyone want to kill people's dogs?

Scout! The thought of someone shooting him was too horrible to imag-ine. Where was he, anyway? Kate's dark brown eyes scoured the camp. There he was! His black nose glistening with growing health, he was nestled in the shadow of their big wagon with both eyes closed as if he didn't have a care in the world. Relief swept through her.

Kate knew her Papa would do something. Jacob Winfield was a good man, and good men didn't let other men shoot family dogs.

From under the wagon's seat Jacob pulled out his rifle. "Let's go," he declared.

The men hadn't been gone five minutes when a rifle shot rang out, followed by the shouts of men's angry voices. Then silence.

The sound of the shots scared Scout awake from his snooze by the wagon. Jumping to his feet, he looked anxiously toward Kate. Fear gripped her heart. "Oh, please, God, don't let them shoot any dogs!" she cried out loud. "Please stop them."

Kate and Jake lay down to sleep in their tent, but Kate tossed and turned so much with worry that the bottom of her bedroll became twisted around her ankles. Every once in a while she poked her head out of the tent to make sure Scout was still tied to the wagon. When would Papa come back?

"You awake, Kate?" Jake wondered aloud as Scout made whimpering sleep noises.

"Yep."

"Papa's been gone a long time."

"Yep."

Kate could hear the rustling of Jake's bedroll as he repositioned himself to face her.

"Think everything's okay?"

"Yep," she replied, although she wasn't so sure.

"You young folks still awake?" It was Papa's voice!

Kate popped up and flipped back the canvas flap of her tent. "What happened, Papa?"

Jake instantly joined her.

"Everything's all right," Papa said, crouching down on his heels by the tent flap. Kate could smell the sweat from his shirt. "Arkansas saved the day, along with Mr. Gantt. Told them the Indians ain't hostile and the dogs ain't a threat. We didn't get 'em stopped before a greenhorn took a shot at one. Fortunately, he missed. Then they finally listened to us."

Jacob stood up, holding his rifle, his knees creaking.

"Papa." Kate's eyes searched her father's face. "Why are people so afraid of the Indians if they're not hostile?"

"Don't know, daughter," Papa replied, "exceptin' that people are usually afraid of things they don't understand."

9

THE MAN IN BLACK

Sunday, June 4

Papa was teaching Kate how to guide an ox team. Since Joshua and Caleb were already trained to voice commands and they were in the lead today, she was walking alongside them holding the riding crop. It was only nine o'clock, but it was already hot. She could feel the sweat starting inside her bonnet and under her arms.

Kate looked up to see a man wearing a black preacher's cloak and a wide-brimmed black hat approaching on horseback. Slowing his spotted gelding's gait to match their strides, he pulled off his hat to reveal long blond hair. He sat straight and tall in the saddle, his horse's reins held loosely in one hand, the other clutching a well-worn Bible. When he smiled and nodded to Kate and her mother, she noticed coffee-colored eyes that radiated kindness.

"Mr. Winfield." His tone was cordial, but his voice had the confidence of a man who often spoke before groups of people. "Might I have a word with you?"

Kate's heart skipped a beat. She was going to be on her own with the oxen team. "Don't worry, Kate," Jacob reassured her. "Pop them on their hindquarters if they amble too far in one direction. Just remember, 'hee' is for right and 'haw' is for left. They'll understand."

With that Papa turned to the rider. "Preacher Garrison, what can I do for you?" Jacob asked, wiping his hands on his muslin vest.

"Sir, I'm asking people what they think about traveling like this on the Sabbath. I'm strongly against it myself, but before I talk to Burnett, I thought I'd find out how you folks feel."

Kate was trying to keep her eyes on the team, but she stole a quick glance at her mother. She knew very well what Mama thought about it, because she had brought it up with Papa this morning, just before a short family worship time.

Sure enough her mother came over to walk beside her husband, her stained apron pinned against her dress by the force of the wind.

"Mr. Garrison." Mama spoke up over the clattering and banging of the wagons. "I feel as strongly as you do about this. The Bible tells us to honor the Sabbath, and that's what I think we should do. Jacob doesn't quite agree."

Papa shook his head. "It's not that I don't agree, Abby. It's that we have to get through the mountains before the first snow, and we're already late."

Mama didn't say any more in front of the preacher, although Kate knew exactly what she wanted to say. Mama had already said it this morning over a cup of coffee. "Jacob, how is God going to honor our trip if we don't honor His Sabbath?"

Kate nudged Caleb to the left a bit and kept walking. The thought that they all needed Joe and his gnarled old wisdom stick right now flitted across her mind.

"Our departure date is a valid concern, Mr. Winfield," the preacher acknowledged. "But I'm inclined to give God the benefit of the doubt. If we honor Him, He'll honor us. May I share what the both of you have said with Mr. Burnett?"

Kate's parents both nodded, and the preacher trotted off.

"Jacob, you and I both know who's behind this traveling on Sundays," Abby began, snatching some yellow prairie wildflowers off their stems as she walked. "It's Eyers."

"Sundays would be an issue on a train like this with or without Eyers, Abby. Let's just trust that God's going to show Burnett what to do."

Kate thought this was wise on her Papa's part. He didn't quote the Bible often, which sometimes bothered Mama, but he lived it. And he had wisdom.

That evening after supper the Winfields were quietly talking around their fire when Lancefield Johnson suddenly came rushing up to them.

"Mrs. Winfield, come quick! Mary Lenox got burnt." Lancefield leaned weakly against a wagon wheel, out of breath.

"Thank you, Mr. Johnson, for fetching me. I'll come directly," Abby said. Turning to Jacob, she added, "I'll take Kate with me."

"Kate, grab my medical bag and let's go."

These were the words Kate loved to hear. Almost from the time they had moved to Missouri, she had been helping her mother and Bessie tend the sick. At first Kate would roll bandages from white tow cloth or hold the thin sharp needles, pour tincture, or simply fetch fresh water. As she grew older, she helped Bessie make the tinctures from the herbs they grew in their vegetable garden. She also read her mother's medical book, the one that Mama carried in the satchel that served as her medical supply kit. But now Kate was quite old enough to start figuring out people's sicknesses.

A few minutes later the two women found the Lenox wagons. The smell of smoke hung over the campsite like a cloud.

Louesa Lenox cradled her daughter's blonde head in her lap and pressed a small cup of water to her lips. Abby quickly took the scissors out of her bag and cut open the child's charred pinafore to expose her burned legs. The other three little sisters huddled next to their Papa, one of them clutching a small gingham doll with burned red yarn hair. The only sound was little Mary's soft moans. Kate's heart went out to this child, who obviously was in great agony.

Abby spoke calmly. "Kate, while I examine Mary, please look after that young man and get him some water. He saved this girl's life!"

Mama turned to the father, whose big arms encircled his other girls. "You did the right thing, Mr. Lenox, by dousing her with water. Her legs are burned badly; this left one's the worst. You'll have to watch the swelling. If that doesn't get too bad, and her lungs don't fill with fluid, I think she'll probably make it. She's in shock, though; you'll have to keep her warm. But this could have been a lot worse," she added.

To Kate's surprise, the young man was the Easterner who had winked at her a few weeks ago. He was straddling a nearby log, holding his elbows on his knees with his arms outstretched. It was the unmistakable look of pain on his face that made Kate look closer. The sleeves of his plaid shirt had been singed almost all the way off and the skin on his exposed arms was red and already swelling and blistering.

"Why, you're burned!" Kate cried with alarm.

"It's not too bad. I'll be all right before too long," he said with a wry smile. He waved off her worry with a hand.

When Kate brought back a cup of water from a barrel near the Lenox's wagon, the stranger introduced himself. "I'm John Prentiss, Miss Winfield."

"How did you know my name?" Kate inquired, as she carefully handed him the cup.

"I made inquiries," John said slyly, looking at her over the cup.

Kate flushed and pointed to his arms. "How did this happen to you?"

"I was on my way to the river," John explained, wincing with pain. "Mary was playing with her doll by the fire. I didn't see her folks anywhere around. I was going on by, but then I suddenly realized that she was too close to the fire. At that very moment her dress caught on fire so I ran over and grabbed her and rolled her in the dirt. I wish I had gotten to her sooner."

Just then Abby spoke up. She was pressing a cool compress against little Mary's forehead. "Mr. Prentiss, you saved Mary's life."

"But she's so badly burned," John replied, clearly distraught over what had happened.

"Mr. Prentiss." Louesa's voice was soft as she stroked her daughter's hair. "We'll never be able to thank you enough for saving her. I'm just sorry you've been hurt, too."

"I'm not hurt too badly, Mrs. Lenox," John replied, as he gave the empty cup back to Kate. "I think the burn only got the first few layers of skin."

Later, around the Winfield campfire, Jacob and Ole Joe were talking about what had happened. John Prentiss had returned to his campsite. His wounds would heal, but he would probably have scars. The same was true for little Mary. She had survived a terrible accident, but she would forever have reminder marks on her left leg.

"It was the Lord who had Mr. Prentiss come by right then," Abby said thoughtfully. "We can all thank Him this whole thing wasn't worse."

Kate found herself deeply impressed by what John had done. It took a man of character to risk being seriously burned to save someone else's life.

10

CAW TROPHIES

Tuesday, June 6

At noon the newly elected captain, Peter Burnett, selected a campsite with no trees. Kate heard some of the men complain about this, but Papa said there weren't that many oases to choose from out here in the wide open spaces.

While they were eating a lunch of cold beans and bacon, Jane suddenly appeared. "Mrs. Winfield, can you come?" Jane's words were clipped as she tried to catch her breath. "Mama sent me to fetch you. Mr. Stewart's wife is doing poorly."

Kate remembered that Mrs. Stewart was expecting a child in early July. "Let me get my bag," Abby replied. "Kate, you come, too."

"She's complaining about her head and an upset stomach," Mr. Stewart told them when they arrived at the Stewart's wagon after a half-mile walk. "She got dizzy an hour ago. She's inside the wagon here."

Mr. Stewart steadied his four mules as Kate and her mother bunched their long calico skirts and petticoats above their knees to climb into the wagon.

Their medical satchel was really pieces of old tapestry that Abby had sewn together into a large bag with a leather handle. Some people called it a carpetbag. The kit was heavy, so Kate set it on the grass while she waited outside with a panting Scout, who had invited himself along.

"Kate, she's got a pretty high fever," Abby announced through the back flaps a few minutes later. "And she seems nervous."

"Should we try echinacea, Mama? Or maybe catnip?"

Her mother smiled, and Kate dug into the bag for bottles of both.

Just as they finished caring for Mrs. Stewart, the afternoon bugle sounded, and the wagons resumed their journey. Kate and Abby and a limping Scout stood facing toward the rear of the column of moving wagons that was now passing them, waiting for Jacob and Old Joe to come by with the Winfield wagons, which were positioned toward the rear of the train today.

With her hands to shield her eyes, Kate squinted, not so much from the sun as from the dust. It was everywhere and coated everything—animals, people, and wagons. It got in her face, in her hair, even in her mouth. The wind, the incessant wind, only made it worse. Did it ever stop blowing out here on the plains?

Kate breathed in dust through her nose and coughed, but the coughing didn't stop the constant tickle down deep in her throat. She longed for a swig of water from the canteen swinging on the side of their wagon.

"I think Mrs. Stewart will be fine," Mama began. "This heat's tough on all of us, but especially on someone with child."

Kate picked a couple of sprigs of available Indian grass to swish the afternoon insects away.

"I'm right proud of you, young lady." Mama threw her right arm around her daughter's shoulders. "You've got a gift for nursing."

Kate beamed. "I like helping people with you, Mama," Kate replied, slapping a cricket off her lavender skirt, which now had a jagged tear in the bottom ruffle, the kind of tear that would be hard to mend.

"Afternoon, ladies. Are we heading in a different direction today?" It was Arkansas's ruddy voice. The mountaineer had trotted up to them and reined his Appaloosa, named Red, to a walk. "Might I suggest we turn around and head toward the west fer awhile?"

Kate liked the old fur trapper a lot. In spite of the fact Arkansas had spent years in the wilderness trapping beaver all by himself, he was polite and seemed to have a sense of humor.

"Saw," Kate spoke in a tone that pretended to be perturbed he had asked something so silly. "You *know* we're waiting for Papa."

"Yer Papa?" Arkansas's eyes twinkled under his bushy eyebrows. "I'm thinkin' he's probly headin' west." The trapper scratched his shabby beard with tobacco stained fingers as if he was trying to figure something out. "Yep, I'm pretty sure I saw 'im and Ole Joe 'while back. They're thinkin' 'bout Oregon if my ole brain serves me right. As I recollect, that's *west* of here."

Kate laughed and so did her Mama. "I hear Oregon Country's a good place," Abby replied, shooing away gnats.

"I hope so," he chuckled, "'cause you all are in fer the journey of your lives t'git there."

Just then Kate caught her mother's elbow. "Mama, look!" she exclaimed in a low voice.

A large group of Indian braves was walking past the wagon train, headed east. A few wore the traditional feathered headdresses with their faces painted in black and red and yellow stripes and their tomahawks and spears glinting in the hot prairie sun. However, the majority of them had been wounded. Some staggered in pairs, their knees buckling under their own weight, while long sharp spears provided makeshift crutches for others. Bloodstained slings supported lifeless arms, and bandages with deep red splotches concealed serious head injuries.

"There must be nearly a hundred of them," Abby commented quietly, as if they might be able to hear her.

"Don't be afraid, Ma'am," Arkansas spoke up through another gust of wind. "They're Caw warriors. Goin' home from a battle with the Pawnee, from the looks of it."

It was then that Kate noticed something else that horrified her. When one of the warriors spotted her, he proudly held up something. It dangled in a clump of long black slimy hair clutched between his bloody fingers. It was a human scalp! Kate's eyes widened in shock. Then another brave thumbed his bead necklace out from his chest to display—a severed finger!

"Trophies, ladies," Arkansas explained as he spurred his horse to ride off. "Those are their trophies."

That night Kate stared into their campfire and thought about the Indians. What kind of people were they—these red men who could help you or scalp you? She found herself drawn to them and yet repulsed by them. This was a strange land, and its inhabitants were even stranger.

11

THE STORM

Tuesday–Thursday, June 6–8

As Kate was drifting off to sleep Tuesday evening, she didn't notice that the crickets in the grasses around the campsites had mysteriously stopped chirping. Neither did she smell the rising moisture in the air, nor hear the first pitter-patter of rain on the top of their canvas tent.

A few hours later she and Jake were awakened by the howling of the wind and the swaying of their tent. Over a sudden clap of thunder, that sounded like it was just overhead, she heard Papa calling.

"Kate! Kate!"

As she pulled back the tent flap her soaking-wet father handed her two pieces of rope. "You and Jake put these around the poles and pull against the wind, or you'll lose the tent!"

For the remainder of a long and horrible night, she and Jake tried to snatch moments of sleep while they held on to their ropes and wrestled with the shrieking wind.

Lightning bolts of electricity, white and jagged, split the sky. Kate could plainly see them through the tent—a maze of frightening light in a prairie of darkness. Thunder exploded in deafening roars, so loud that Kate wanted to let go of her rope to put her fingers in her ears.

Between thunderclaps Kate could hear cries of dismay and frustration coming from all the families around them, as the storm attacked the wagon train, seemingly determined to blow over as many tents and wagons as it could.

When the morning light finally came, there was hardly enough of it to see by. Heavy black clouds hung so low that Kate felt like she could have touched them, and they continued to disgorge torrents of water.

"Joe! There's no point in trying to move today!" Jacob was yelling back toward the supply wagon through sheets of rain that sliced at his face. Kate realized that the rain was preventing the emigrants from even lighting a fire. The water was already standing at least four inches deep in the campsites. Everyone would be eating cold food.

She remembered bad storms back in Missouri. Strong winds would whip around their house, tearing off shutters and uprooting bushes. But, here on the prairie, this storm seemed worse than those back home. Here, there were no trees or buildings to offer protection, and the winds shrieked at them in a pandemonium of terrifying sounds. They were at the mercy of the storm, and it kept coming without any letup.

"Mistah Jacob!" Joe's already raspy voice was hoarse from hollering so much. "She's stuck again."

Not again!

It was Thursday. After two days and nights of rain, the water-soaked ground had become a quagmire of thick reddish-brown mud that could devour a wagon wheel up to its axle within seconds. It was as if the earth were ravenous and couldn't get enough. They had tried to move the wagons that morning, but over and over the wheels kept getting stuck. They had only come a few hundred yards from last night's camp.

"Whoa!" Jacob grabbed the huge crooked horns on Balaam's head, and the team gratefully stood still. "We can't get anywhere in this mud," Jacob said in a disgusted tone. "We're just going to have to camp right where we are and wait until it stops raining."

The animals didn't like the rain any more than Kate and her family did. For the last two nights, they had thronged together looking for safety in numbers, yearning for a barn and stalls. Kate remembered the sight of a dead cow that had been struck by lightning, lying stiffly in the mud, the rain pelting its body as if to clean the carcass before the vultures got to it. Folks everywhere were out searching in the pouring rain for horses and cattle that had stampeded away, frightened by the thunder.

So far, the Winfields hadn't lost any of their livestock. At least not yet. Yesterday, Papa had given Jake the responsibility of keeping an eye out for straying cattle. Banding together with Warren and Elisha in what they called their "Cattle Recovery Mission," the muddy and rain-soaked boys relayed information back to headquarters throughout the day, accompanied by their trusty cattle-hunting dog, Scout. Although the Winfield and Applegate cattle were nervous and skittish, they had remained with the herd.

The drooping brim of Kate's sunbonnet was of no help now. She slogged toward Papa in the deep water, the hem of her lavender skirt permanently stained in mud. "Papa, I can help!" she screamed.

"Try to keep these animals calm, Kate," Jacob said, as he sloshed back toward the supply wagon. "I'll help Joe."

The oxen's flanks were quivering while long streams of water trickled down their crusty colored snouts and off their black nostrils. Their droopy eyes literally begged Kate to get them out of the mess, both the rain and the mud. "It's all right, boy," she said to Balaam in as calm a tone as she could muster through the wind. "Everything's going to be all right."

"Abby, see if you can't wedge the plank under the back wheel again." Papa's tense voice carried through the rain.

Kate rubbed the thin cloth of her linen jacket, shivering in the cold. How had it come to this? No one ever told them the prairie could be this awful. There was her Mama, working like a man, drenched from bonnet to boot. And Papa! The mud sucked at his boots like quicksand each time he took a step from one wet hole to another.

And Joe? While their faithful hand was never one to complain, even he was having a hard time maintaining a positive attitude in the midst of it all. "Must be the Lord's way of slowin' us down," was about all he'd said. Kate wasn't sure if he was trying to convince others or himself when he said it.

Right now, the muscles in Joe's stout shoulders bulged through his drenched white muslin shirt as he crouched down on his knees to help Mama ram the board under the stuck wheel. Years of life on the farm had made Joe very strong, but he was aging and tasks like this took a lot of strength.

"Ye got it, Miz Abby," Joe declared. "Now, hold it right there."

"Ready, Joe? On three, let's heave." Papa took a deep breath.

Kate rubbed Balaam's snout. She was worried. The wagon was still chocked full of heavy supplies. They had packed forty pounds of tenting, sixty pounds of bedding, and two hundred pounds of personal baggage on the small wagon. It also held their keg of pickles and two hundred pounds of beans, not to mention the yards of coiled rope. There was even more in there that she couldn't remember. The supply wagon was very heavy, and Papa and Joe were getting ready to lift the back left corner all by themselves.

"One . . . two . . . three!"

The two men lifted the wagon up and Abby jammed the log under the wheel as fast as she could.

It was done, but it was obvious that if they kept on trying to move the wagons, they would get stuck over and over.

Just then John Gantt appeared, riding down the length of the columns and yelling to the men to form circles with nearby wagons and stay where they were until the ground dried. The drenched wagons began pulling into haphazard corrals, everyone thankful to stop fighting the mud.

12

AFTER THE STORM

Friday, June 9

On Friday the wagon train only managed to travel a few miles before the nooning. As soon as they stopped, the sun finally came out; so John Gantt made the decision to camp right there for the night, and let the women use the afternoon sun to begin the overwhelming job of drying everything out.

And it was everything—every linen sack filled with beans or cornmeal, every quilt, every bedroll, every article of clothing—they were all soaked.

Kate found that the bows of bent hickory wood supporting the cotton bonnet were as wet as the top itself. *I hope they'll dry out without cracking,* she thought with an audible sigh. Grandpa Winfield's plantation desk was already outside, its pigeonhole cubbies empty of everything, including Mama's damp Bible, which lay open in the sun. Their heavy wooden trunk was already outside too. Against the beveled baseboard lay the disheveled patchwork quilt, smelling like it had been cooped up in a musty basement.

The wagon groaned as Kate climbed in her bare feet around two damp cotton food sacks, one with coffee and the other with sugar. She noticed that these sacks were smaller than when she and Joe had first loaded them. The same was true of their fruit preserves—only six wax-sealed quarts left now. Not quite three weeks on the trail, and already their supplies were noticeably dwindling.

"Kate, check the gourd!" Mama's voice carried over the background of people talking, oxen lowing, and mules braying for their supper. Kate clambered over to retrieve the gourd from the pocket painstakingly sewn onto the inside of the wagon's top. She hesitated before pulling out the corn cob stopper, afraid of what she would find. If the seed coats were wet, the small embryos would break through the coats and germinate, but without soil they would quickly die. How would they be able to start a new life in Oregon without seed?

Kate twisted the stopper up, then yanked it out. Holding her breath, she poured a few kernels into the palm of her hand. There were the wheat seeds and the tan barley seeds, some pumpkin seeds, and even their flax. And . . . each one was dry to her touch!

Elated, Kate funneled the seeds back into the gourd, popped in the stopper, and climbed out through the puckered opening. "Mama, they didn't get wet!" Kate exclaimed.

"Oh, thank God!" her mother responded. "I don't know what we would do if our seed got ruined."

"I wish you hadn't quit, Burnett." Papa was draping a coarse piece of damp char cloth over a flint to start Mama's cooking fire.

"I got a wife and six children to take care of, Jacob." Peter Burnett mopped back some strings of blond hair from his lined forehead. "I got fed up with the complaining. Did you hear about the fight?" Burnett didn't wait for an answer. "Two men actually fought over hanging clothes lines between the wagons. If it isn't the rain, it's the heat. If it isn't the heat, it's the guard duty. Why, Eyers even complained last night because he had to pitch his tent in the mud!"

Jacob laid the char wrapped flint on some shredded hemp rope then began to strike it at an angle with a sharp piece of steel. The steel cut through the char, and soon a few sparks were flying. But no fire.

"I must admit," Papa said as he started the process again. "The idea of dividing into two columns is probably a good one, Peter. It should be easier to travel with fewer wagons."

"Trouble is, I'm not sure some folks are willing to obey anybody. We've got no community out here, unless it's a few small groups that seem to have made friends." Burnett brushed his chin just under his unkempt whiskers. "William Martin took over for me with the Light Column. And Lindsey's brother, Jesse, agreed to captain your Cow Column. He'll get it organized and probably split it up into smaller companies. Most of you will probably be passing us within a few days in spite of your five thousand head." To that, Burnett let out a short laugh.

Handing the gourd to her mother, Kate said, "I sure hope we don't see Mr. Eyers anytime soon."

Abby shook her head sadly. "I'm afraid he's the type that looks for trouble, Kate," she replied.

13

INDIAN!

Saturday, June 10

Nearly three weeks had passed since they left Independence, and the wagon train was rumbling along beside the Little Blue, a quiet bubbling river that flowed from the northwest. Following it upriver would soon lead them to an even longer river called the Platte. The high dry grasslands along the river—which wasn't really blue at all—ushered the emigrants into a world unlike anything Kate had ever known.

Here the sky ended only because it met the horizon and the prairie opened into a panorama of tall green grasses and beautiful wildflowers as far as the eye could see. Walking beside the wagons, the emigrants could not always see over the tops of the six- or eight-foot tall prairie grasses. But, at the noonings and in the evening camps, Kate loved to perch up on the wagon seat and watch the wind make waves through the grasses as if the prairie were a great ocean.

"I think God's smiling on His creation today, Joe," she remarked. Dry ground and a change of clothes had helped Kate feel better since yesterday. Her yellow plaid skirt billowed out with each step as they traveled through more miles of flat fertile plains and prairie grasses. *Dry* prairie grasses.

"That's fer sure, Missy." Joe's crooked but white teeth shone against his black face. "God does a good job of creatin' things."

Kate detected a twinkle in his eye. "What, Joe?" she asked.

"This Louisiana Purchase place is mighty big, 'specially when ye're walkin' it." The squawks of a huge covey of white snow geese with black-tipped wings nearly drowned him out.

"Yep," she replied, eyeing the huge fluffy white clouds stacked on top of one another, like castles in the sky. "And we're walking it, step by step."

For a moment she thought about all the steps she had taken. They were already more than the stars in the sky, she was sure, and the train hadn't even reached the Continental Divide. "Papa says that a man named Zebulon Pike explored this area and called it 'the Great American Desert.'" Kate added, "Doesn't look like a desert to me, Joe."

"No, more like God's country, Missy," he offered. "This river sure does sing His praises."

Lined by deep green hardwood trees, the Little Blue teemed with life. Chunky pheasants with bronze heads and dark brown feathers pranced on the banks. Quails called out their names: "Bob-white!" A "two pointer," a male deer with two points on his antlers, had strolled by early yesterday morning. And Captain Gantt even spotted a buffalo, an old male who had wandered off from his herd, roaming alone on a ridge.

"Good eating coming up soon," Papa had said, pointing at him. "Let's hope our hunters find them and bring us back a supply."

Joe's perspective had been a bit different. "They will. It's God's provision for us, Mistah Jacob," he had said.

This was something Kate loved about Joe. The old black man had a way of finding God in every part of life. While she had been admiring the scenery and Papa had been thinking about food, Joe had been silently giving God the praise for creating all this.

"Deserts? Are ye talking about deserts?" The dust flew around Jake's dark breeches as he bounded up to Joe. "I hear there's Indians in these deserts."

"There aren't any Indians, Jake," Kate countered, catching her bonnet in the wind.

"Is, too," Jake retorted, jutting out his chin. "Warren and Elisha's Papa saw one."

"Now when did you hear 'bout that, Mistah Jake?" Joe asked, hawing Caleb toward the left.

"This morning. Was a dead body. All cut up." Jake waved a hand holding an imaginary knife. "Mr. Applegate saw it. Said it was missin' some parts."

Kate instantly recalled the human scalp and finger. "Did he know why?" Kate asked, almost afraid of the answer.

"Yep. Said it was a Pawnee. Must have met up with that war-party we seen awhile back. And he said another thing too." Jake's thumbs pulled at his cowhide brown suspenders as he rambled on. "Said them Indians are gonna steal us blind, if we don't watch out."

Joe must have seen the deep creases of worry now lining Kate's forehead under her sunbonnet. "Now don't ye go worryin', Missy," he told her. "This might be Indian Territory, but yer Papa and the others are keepin' a good lookout."

That night, in spite of Joe's words, Kate couldn't sleep. She was bothered by what Jake had heard, so she decided to slip away from the campsite and visit Papa, who was on guard duty.

The stars created a twinkling tapestry above her. She loved the stars, because gazing at them made whatever problems she had seem smaller. After all, if God was big enough to create such glory in the heavens, He could certainly take care of her worries. Tonight, however, the problem didn't seem small—the Indians might do them harm.

She was beginning to wonder why in the world they were making this trip. What could Papa have been thinking? It was dangerous out here. *I could have been home,* she thought, *safely tucked in my soft feather bed, concerned only about the Sunday picnic tomorrow and what Jack might say about me to my friend, Jenny.*

But out here there were worries, many of them: people at odds, perilous river crossings, awful storms, food supplies that were already beginning to run low, and now—Indians. Growing anxieties had begun nibbling at her soul like rats munching cheese. Faith and hope were hard things to hang on to, she thought, especially when things start to go wrong.

As she passed the last set of tents, the mournful howls of distant coyotes sounded even closer. Kate shivered.

With the light of the moon and the stars to guide her, she lifted her petticoat above her ankles so she wouldn't trip on the woody plants that were scattered about. Her bare feet were calloused and used to hiking, but Kate didn't want another tear in her skirt. She had only brought two skirts, and her other one had been nearly ruined during the storm.

The high chirping of night crickets mingled with the howls of distant coyotes as Kate approached the large meadow. She could hear the gentle chewing sounds of the cattle grazing on Indian grass and wheat grass.

Within a few steps, Kate heard men's voices. She slowed down.

"Keep your rifle handy," one was saying.

"It's handy. I got me a Springfield before I came on this trip, and I like it right well. Keep a sharp eye out for thieving Indians, Jacob."

Papa!

"I'm hoping there won't be any, John," Papa replied.

All of a sudden a gunshot exploded in the darkness. "Indian!" someone hollered from across the field. "A thieving Indian!"

"Did you get 'im?" one of the guards shouted.

"Couldn't tell," came back the reply. "Let's go see."

Kate decided this was no place for a young woman, so she quickly fled back to camp, the shot ringing in her ears.

Her sleep was fitful, harassed by dreams of stealthy Indians creeping toward her tent.

14

THE PHILADELPHIAN

Sunday, June 11

The notes of the morning bugle aroused Kate out of her uneasy slumber and ushered in her first waking thought: What happened last night? Did the guard shoot an Indian? With her head throbbing from lack of sleep, she pushed open the tent flap to ask Papa, but he was nowhere in sight.

Oh well, she sighed to herself, *it will just have to wait. Meanwhile I'd better get on with my first chore—milking Tess.* Kate woke up Jake and sent him out to fetch more driftwood for the fire, and then she untied Scout from his accustomed place under the supply wagon. She noticed as he trotted after Jake that his limp was not as bad; his leg seemed to be healing nicely.

While Tess munched on some grass, Kate rested her weary head on the cow's flank. She had done this chore so many times that she could do it in her sleep. After cleaning the udder, she placed the empty pail under the cow and squeezed her fingers in sequence from top down to mimic the sucking movement of a calf. Three gallons a day from Tess was providing fresh milk in the mornings and thick warm buttermilk at night.

Thoughts of last night plunged into her mind like milk into the bucket. Had the Indians really been there? Where was Papa? Was it bad that they hadn't heard any news?

The milk sloshed in the pail as Kate lugged it toward the fire.

"Miz Abby." Joe stepped over the wagon tongue from inside the corral. His shuffle seemed more pronounced this morning. "We best watch our flour. Don't know when we can get some more."

Abby nodded in agreement as Kate set the milk pail down.

"Milk, Joe?" Mama asked as she scooped out a fresh cupful.

Just as she ladled herself a cup of Tess's fresh milk Papa appeared, accompanied by John Prentiss. Today John wore a dark green shirt with his sleeves rolled up to his elbows, showing burn marks that were not yet healed. Wide suspenders held up his gray breeches, and he carried a rifle in his left hand. John's chiseled features seemed tired, and his wavy chestnut hair was flat from a night under his wide brimmed hat, which Kate observed when he politely whisked it off.

"John, you know my wife, Abby, and my daughter, Kate," Jacob said, over the crowing of a rooster. "But I don't think you've met my son Jake and my hired man Joe."

"Glad to make your acquaintance, gentlemen," the young man replied, shaking hands with Joe and Jake. Mama was cooking breakfast over a fire of driftwood that Jake had collected along the river bank last night. Joe had dug a trench for the fire, because they had quickly learned that cooking fires had to be sheltered from the constant wind. Thankfully the smells of coffee brewing and bacon frying overcame the sweat and animal smells from Papa and John.

"Mr. Prentiss, can you eat with us?" Kate inquired.

"That'd surely be nice, Mrs. Winfield. Truth is, I haven't had a decent cooked meal in awhile. Traveling with men isn't quite the same as having a woman around."

"I understand your traveling companions are from the east." Abby spooned some strawberry preserves on top of the johnnycakes.

"Yes, Ma'am. Mr. Osborne and I call Philadelphia home. Mr. Johnson and Mr. Atkins come from Boston. Douglas and I actually met Lancefield and Jeremiah in Independence and decided to travel together from there."

"I'm supposing you're heading for Oregon?"

"Yes, Ma'am," the visitor replied, a plate full of johnnycakes and bacon now in his hands.

"Guard duty was a comedy of errors last night, Abby." Jacob settled down on a plank set between two stumps and motioned for John to do the same.

"First, Prentiss here got me itchy 'bout Indians. Then Nate Sutton shoots one, or so we thought." Jacob carefully sipped his hot coffee. "Turns out the 'Indian' was actually the Martin brothers' prize mule from Kentucky." Neither Papa nor John could hide their smiles. "Nate's bullet ended up being a $300 shot. They're burying the poor animal right now."

Kate was sorry about the mule but relieved to hear that there had been no Indians. "Mr. Prentiss, do you own cattle?" she inquired as she dished three hot johnnycakes onto another tin plate.

"No, Ma'am, I don't," he responded. "But when I came on this trip, I agreed to help with the herd, because I'd like to learn more about cattle. This is my chance."

"I think this trip is a learning experience for all of us," Abby replied. "Won't you stay for a short service with us after breakfast, Mr. Prentiss? It's Sunday, you know." Mama's tone had a hint of disapproval because they were still traveling on the Sabbath.

"Thank you, Ma'am," John replied. "But I've got chores back at the campsite, and by the look of the sun, we should be heading out soon."

15

SCOUT ALERT

Sunday, June 11

Kate's thoughts about the visitor quickly faded as the oxen heaved and the wagons pulled out. By noon, fatigue had settled in and Kate was happy to rest not only her weary feet but also her tired body.

"Kate, Joe says we've walked eight miles this morning," Jake announced. The packs he had just unloaded from Midnight were piled near the grazing horse. "I think I'm gonna go out and catch me an antelope. Joe's coming. You want to come, too?"

As tired as she was, Kate thought that watching Jake trying to catch an antelope would be something to see, something that would definitely lighten her sagging spirits.

The antelope had been everywhere this morning. The furry horned animals with their long legs and short tails gracefully bounded across the prairie like big rabbits. With eyes on the sides of their heads, they stopped and watched the passing emigrants as much as the emigrants watched them.

"Joe, where's your wisdom stick and pipe today?" The youngster squared his straw hat and forged a path through some tall grass toward a level plain not far from the campsite.

"I believes I plum forgot 'em, Mistah Jacob," Joe replied, hobbling around a clump of switch grass. "Wrapped 'em with my tent, I reckon."

"We might be needing some of that wisdom, Joe." Kate whisked a bright orange dragonfly off her skirt. "I hear antelope are pretty smart creatures. They can smell a dangerous animal from a long distance and hear him, too."

"Be quiet then," Jake admonished, fanning some gnats away from his face with his hat. "We don't want to scare them."

Within a few minutes Scout's nose was pinned to the ground. The dog had picked up a scent that led him scurrying out toward the plain. All of a sudden Scout spotted the culprit, and with a burst of speed he galloped full speed toward his prey. Kate had known he had it in him, but watching him run made her heart leap. Almost four weeks had passed since the whipping, and there was no sign of the injury. Faster and faster he went, all four legs carrying his lean muscular body in long strides, his fluffy black tail flying in the wind.

"Look, he's going to catch him!" Jake exclaimed.

Scout must have thought so too, for when he got within a few yards of the antelope, the dog yelped with glee.

No sooner had the bark come out of Scout's mouth, when the startled antelope took off like it had been shot from a cannon. Kate could barely believe her eyes. How could any animal accelerate that fast? Joe later maintained that the antelope had bolted fifty yards before he could see the dust behind it.

With his long tongue hanging out, Scout skidded to an abrupt halt in the grass, looking at the fleeing antelope. By this time Kate had untied the sash of her bonnet and tugged it off in delight, and Joe and Jake were slapping their hands on their knees with glee. Poor Scout just could not understand why he hadn't caught the animal. Soon he came trotting back to them, panting with fatigue and wearing such an ashamed look of failure on his face that they all laughed again.

"I'm guessin' he won't be chasin' any more antelope," Joe remarked on their way back.

"Not anytime soon," Kate agreed with a chuckle.

16

WATER

Sunday, June 18

"Can't we fill up more than one barrel?" Jake pleaded, clutching the cow-skin canteen Papa had just handed him. "I'm gonna get thirsty."

"Jake, Joshua's already showing signs of strain," Papa replied, ladling water from the bottom of their supply wagon barrel into the canteen strapped around his neck. "A full water barrel weighs at least fifty pounds, and we need to take that extra weight off him and the other oxen." Papa plugged the container's opening. "Thirty-five miles is a long way between rivers, but we'll fill the canteens and ration how much we drink. We can do this."

"I hope Gantt knows what he's doing, taking us this way," Abby muttered, as she and Kate heaved the rocking chair onto the back of the wagon.

The hemp rope felt rough in Kate's hands as she helped her Mama securely tie up the rocking chair this morning. Mama's rocker had come all the way from Virginia and now it was going all the way to Oregon. It was an heirloom, handed down to Abby by her mother. The spindle-back rocker, made out of mahogany, had been built by Mama's great grandfather and was one of her most precious possessions. One day it would be Kate's.

Kate thought about the trip ahead of them over the next two days. The emigrants had to stay close to the rivers in order to have water for themselves and the animals. Today they would be traveling away from the Little Blue River toward the Platte, thirty-five miles without water. So far, on their best days, they had managed twenty miles, but most of the time it was fifteen or sixteen. Two days without water was pushing the limits for both people and animals, and everyone was anxious about it.

Kate hung her canteen around her neck and called to her brother. "Jake, would you like to know where we're going?"

"I suppose," he said without enthusiasm. "Well," said his sister, trying to encourage him. "We've already crossed the Kansas River and the Little Blue. Now we've got to get to the Platte by crossing a piece of land. The Platte will lead us to where it forks and then we'll follow the North Platte River."

"That sounds like an awful long way to go," Jake whined. "And I can't even see exceptin' where the wagon is. The grass is too tall."

"Ye might try standin' on top of Midnight once in a while, Jake," Joe offered as he stomped out the fire with his boots, leaving the smell of charred wood chips in the air. "That'll git ye above the grass."

"Nah, he won't stand still. Besides, my feet hurt." Jake wiggled his dusty right boot for effect. He was in a bad mood this morning.

Kate went on. "Mine do, too, Jake, but we got to go on. Arkansas says we'll come to a river called the Sweetwater."

"Maybe its water is really sweet, Jake," Abby chimed in, trying to help. Jake perked up slightly. "Like sugar water?"

"Maybe."

Kate continued. "He said that the Sweetwater takes us to the Green River and then we'll get to the Bear and then to the Snake. Understand? Many rivers to follow."

Jake's bottom lip protruded over his top. "We'll *never* get to Oregon."

Kate could feel the exasperation rising up in her throat. She felt like lashing out at her little brother. After all, she had been walking too for the last four weeks. They all had. Her face was sunburned in spite of the wide brim of her sunbonnet, and her hands resembled a cow's hide. Her boots had shrunk in the rain, making them tight. She was cooking over an open fire every night and smelled like a rancid combination of smoke and sweat and dust. She hadn't washed her clothes yet, not even once. And she could never be alone. Even bathing meant other women were around to guard you.

Jake understood none of this. What did he have to whine about? His chores were easy: searching for firewood, keeping the cattle moving, dumping the chamber pot. He actually had time to play with Warren and Elisha at noon or in the evening. Kate didn't have time for anything but work . . .

"Jake—" Joe's deep tone interrupted her thoughts. The black man's large hand patted the ten-year-old on one shoulder. "Why don't we be thankin' the Almighty that we got water to drink. Won't do no good to complain. We got a long journey and that's that." With that Joe heaved the empty water barrel onto the supply wagon.

"I don't feel like bein' thankful," the youngster announced, kicking the dust.

"That's the time to do it anyway," replied Ole Joe wisely. "When we're thankful, the Lord starts bringin' good things our way." The black man expertly cinched the last clove hitch knot that tied down the wagon's bonnet.

Several hours later Kate's eyes were burning from the blinding glare in the cloudless sky and her throat was parched.

"Look, Missy, that's what I meant!" Ole Joe pointed ahead.

As they came up over a slight rise, Kate saw patches of colored wildflowers ahead of them and on the hillsides everywhere she looked. Joe had been right, Kate thought. It was as if a loving Creator had responded to their conversation by taking giant paintbrushes and splashing lavender beardtongue, yellow compass flowers, gold coneflowers, and pink bergamot among the purple Indian grass and green switch grass. Even the bees, buzzing among the petals, didn't bother her. The sight was breathtaking.

As Papa guided the oxen through the wildflowers, Jake noticed Arkansas motioning to them. "Papa," he called from his position beside Balaam, "Arkansas wants us to noon over there with him."

Papa's riding stick flicked Balaam on the hindquarters. "Haw, boys!" he ordered. "Time fer lunch." The oxen's tongues were hanging out. They were ready for the noonin', too.

Just then Jake swirled around on his heels. "Papa, when are we gonna see the elephants?" he asked seriously, walking backwards and facing his father.

"What in the world makes you think we'll be seeing elephants out here?" Papa responded as he flicked Balak to keep him moving with Balaam.

"Joshua says so."

"Why don't you ask Arkansas? He might know," Papa suggested, the hairs of his black mustache, with its hints of silver, spreading apart in a smile.

17

ELEPHANTS?

Sunday, June 18

Later, while their animals grazed, the family ate lunch with Arkansas. Edward Stevenson and his wife Catherine had parked their wagon close by.

All of a sudden Mr. Stevenson's two huge mastiffs with silver colored heads and black muzzles romped over to the Winfields' camp. Ever vigilant Scout took a look at the two powerful dogs and immediately beat a hasty retreat to the bushy Indian grass behind a wagon wheel. Then he growled, low and long. The mastiffs ignored him.

"You got yourself a good guard dog there, Miss Kate." Arkansas chuckled.

Crumbs of cornbread littered the old trapper's thick gray beard. He wiped his mouth with the sleeves of his navy plaid flannel shirt, the same shirt he had been wearing the entire trip. Most of the crumbs remained.

Within moments, a whistle from Mr. Stevenson called his dogs back and rescued Scout, whose eyes had assumed a pitiful look.

"Scout, you can come out now," Kate offered. Scout wasn't dumb, and though he might chase cattle and antelope, he wasn't going to tangle with those big brutes.

"Those dogs are big, but elephants are a lot bigger." Jake slurped up his last bite of molasses pudding. "Arkansas, when are we gonna see the elephants?"

The burly mountain man cocked his wavy head to one side and raised a bushy eyebrow. "Elephants?" he asked.

"Yep. Joshua says we should be seeing them soon." Kate's brother was quite certain about this truth. "Papa didn't know for sure, so he told me to ask you."

Arkansas thoughtfully picked a piece of switch grass for a toothpick.

"Well, young Jake, I wasn't figurin' on any elephants."

"Aw, you know everything about the trail. I'll bet you've seen elephants out here somewhere. Josh says so."

The sliver of switch grass slid to the other side of Arkansas' mouth. "Well, now, jes' maybe yer onto somethin'." The mountain man nodded his head and pulled his chair closer to Jake. "If you folks don't mind, I'll tell the boy a story."

Kate finished her last spoonful of pudding, set her plate on the ground, and listened with her chin in one hand.

"A farmer, prob'ly from Missouri like you, Jake, heard that a circus was in town," Arkansas began. "He wanted to see some elephants, so he hitches up his two horses and loads his wagon with vegetables for market. On the way he met the circus parade, and ye know what? A big elephant is leadin' it. Well, the farmer's right happy 'bout this, but his horses ain't. No siree. They was so scared that they jumped, overturned the wagon, and ruined the vegetables."

"What happened to the farmer?" Jake asked, leaning forward intently.

"Said he didn't mind too much," Arkansas explained, "cause he had 'seen the elephant.'" The last three words came out very slowly with a decided mountain man accent.

Kate wasn't sure how this story applied to Jake's question until Arkansas went on.

"Ye see, Jake." Arkansas slowly got to his feet. "Travelin' in the wilderness is full of dangers and troubles, just like the farmer who lost his vegetables. Some folks who've gone a'fore us call these dangers 'seein' the elephant.'"

"You mean like Indians?" Jake's interest was piqued.

"Could be. But more like hard times—sickness, animals dyin', and such." Arkansas tightened the cinch on Red's black saddle. "I'm hopin' we don't see no elephants on this trip."

"I'll be prayin' 'bout that, Mr. Arkansas," Joe responded as he relit his corncob pipe one last time. "Prayin' hard, I'm thinking.'"

That evening the flickering light from their candles threw moving shadows on the walls of Kate and Jake's tent as they got ready for bed.

Kate's spirits were low, even though they had traveled almost twenty miles that day. Her hair was matted and felt grubby. Her petticoat, once a beautiful crisp white, was now a dingy gray. She felt filthy all over, and she was tired—bone tired—from walking.

And walking.

And walking.

And more than fifteen hundred miles of the two thousand-mile trek to Oregon still lay ahead of them. All afternoon, as she had walked by the wagon, Arkansas's words about "seeing the elephant" kept coming back to her. Now, as she lay her head down, worry began to creep into her heart.

18

KATE'S SECRET

Tuesday, June 20

Folks, looks like we got us another group of wagons fer a spell. Appears they's goin' to California." Arkansas gulped a last sip of coffee and handed the cup to Abby. "They'll be the first to go there with wagons, like we're the first fer Oregon."

"Are they gonna follow us along this here Platte River, Mr. Arkansas?" Joe asked as he dabbed ointment around Midnight's eyes to keep the flies away.

"They'll prob'ly come with us as far as the South Platte, Joe. I'm thinkin' they'll split off thar."

"This is a mighty brown river," Jake offered, as he dug his boots into the muddy bank.

"Right ye are, boy. We trappers say it's upside down—mud on the top. We've been followin' the Platte, which means flat, fer many years." Arkansas hoisted himself up into his saddle. "It's actually two rivers that come together a couple days' ride upriver from here, and then these here waters travel pretty straight, 'bout three hundred miles all the way back to the Missouri."

Kate was always amazed at how much knowledge the old mountain man had gathered, even though he couldn't read a word.

This river was flat all right, very flat. At points its waters actually spilled out over the low banks and covered the land for a mile across, forming a flowing swamp that in many places was only six inches deep.

Today the sand felt grainy under Kate's bare feet. While Arkansas talked, she had buried her toes down deep, hoping for a cool spot. With no trees in sight, the south bank was hot under the noonday sun.

"See you later!" Jake yelled as Arkansas galloped away.

"Look at that." Kate pointed toward a long island in the middle of the river. A huge black bird with a white head and yellow hooked beak was soaring into the clear blue sky. The bird hovered for a second, its wingspan at least seven feet, gave a shrill high-pitched cry, and then suddenly dove into the water. The flopping fish had no chance against the bird's sharp talons. "It's an American Eagle!"

Kate marveled at the majestic beauty of America's national bird.

"Ouch!" The heavy chamber pot settled into the sand when Jake set it down and grabbed his bare toe. "Another prickly pear!" he grimaced. Balancing himself against the wagon, Jake stuck out his dirty bare foot. The sharp point of one of the plant's hazardous needles had punctured his big toe.

"Can I help you, Jake?" Jane had just strolled up to their wagon. Her peacock-blue skirt wrinkled as she bent down to his level. "Got one myself this morning tromping in the sand," she consoled him, pulling out the needle. "Not looking where I was going. It really hurt."

"Them spikes ain't any good fer the animals either," Ole Joe added. Midnight's muzzle flew up in the air as he stomped his front hoof in agreement. "Seems Midnight's wantin' me to check his hooves more often," smiled Joe, patting the packhorse on its withers.

The afternoon was long and lazy, and both animals and people got drowsy in the warm summer sun. The cloth bonnets swayed with the motion of wagons that ambled along the river valley as far as Kate could see. Every few miles Papa would drift off to sleep on his feet, so Mama kept elbowing him good-naturedly in the side. The oxen looked droopy eyed, towing their loads slowly through the dusty grass. Midnight's hooves shuffled in an easy rhythm. Even Scout sauntered leisurely in the shade of the wagons, trying to conserve his energy.

"Kate, I have something to tell you." Jane's voice was almost a whisper. She fingered a blonde curl near her cheek as she walked along with her friend.

"What is it?" Kate asked.

"William Vaughn's been asking me to walk with him. Two times now." Jane adjusted her quilted blue bonnet. Her cheeks almost glowed.

"The man who almost drowned?"

"Yep. First, he asked Father. Then, last night he asked me."

"Did you go?"

"Yes, silly. Of course I went. It was nice." Jane's lifted her cotton skirt like a fan and began to sway from side to side. "I think I like him."

Kate twirled her own yellow plaid skirt in response to her friend. "Jane, I hope he's the one for you," she sparkled. "Wouldn't that be something—to find your beau on this wagon train!"

Kate had never really had a steady beau. Not a serious one anyway. Oh, Jack Stewart had been interested in her back home, but Kate was leaving. And that was that. Many women Kate's age were already married with children. Marriage was in Kate's future, or so she hoped, but she felt like she wanted to do something else first.

And this was Kate's secret. Something deep inside her, what Mama called a "still small voice," was pulling at her. She didn't really understand it—it wasn't really a voice at all. It was more like a longing.

She was only able to talk about it once with her mother.

"I want to do what you do, Mama," Kate had told her one night on their way back from helping a neighbor. "Only I want to do more."

"You can do more, Kate. You can do anything you want to do."

"I know men can be doctors, Mama. But can women?" she finally asked. "Could I be a doctor and help people?"

Kate remembered the croaking frogs from that night and the smell of the spring night air. Abby's face had been hidden by her stiff slatted bonnet, but Kate remembered every word her Mama had said.

"With God all things are possible, my girl." Mama's words carried a sense of conviction. "Don't let anyone stand in the way of your dream. God will work it out."

"What about Papa?" Kate had asked as the buggy had bumped along the road toward home. "He doesn't agree." This was true. Although Jacob loved his daughter very much, he wanted her to do what "all well-bred Christian young ladies should do" and that was to become someone's wife and mother. While he supported his wife with her midwifery and had allowed Kate to learn nursing skills from Abby and Bessie, doctoring was "a man's job," and that was that.

That night, as they had passed a barred owl hooting in a dark oak tree along the road, Abby had leaned toward her daughter. "If God can change the hearts of kings, He can work on your Papa's heart, Kate. If this is from God, He'll see that it happens."

This was Kate's dream. That night with her mother she had embraced the hope that someday God would let her, a woman, become a doctor. And that her father, a nineteenth-century farmer from Missouri, would give his blessing when she did.

19

THE STRANGER

Tuesday, June 20

Unlike their calm and drowsy afternoon, however, evening at the camp-site was anything but quiet. The Cow Column had actually passed the Light Column, and Kate could hear men throughout the camp congratulating one another. "Why, Jesse will have us beating them to Oregon if we keep this up!" Edward Stevenson yelled to Papa as they corralled the wagons.

The cattle, sensing the excitement, mooed loudly. Chains clanked when the men tossed them near their wagon tongues for the night. Hammers pounded against wooden stakes for tents.

As the men were finishing up their hard work for the day, the women were just beginning theirs. That was life on the trail—the women's work began when the western horizon reflected the oranges and blues of sunset. Tonight was no exception.

Chickens fluttered in their cages, squawking to get out. Hungry toddlers in short dresses cried, demanding dinner. And Scout sat in front of Kate, expectantly thumping his tail on the ground, waiting for supper.

"Scout, you'll get your plate when I get mine," Kate scolded him, as she lifted Midnight's packsaddle off the draft horse. It felt unusually heavy tonight, she thought, and let it fall with a crash onto the ground.

Scout's tail whacked at the ground even harder.

"Scout, *be patient*! I'll feed you when we eat."

Midnight's flanks were wet from sweat under his blanket, Kate discovered, as she gently brushed the dirt off his hindquarters. The draft horse softly snorted his contentment.

She hadn't quite finished when Scout crouched down and started growling. With one hand on Midnight to keep him calm, Kate pivoted around. A stranger appeared on foot, silhouetted against the rusts and violets of the western sky. A wide-brimmed hat, a black suit, a black ascot tied under a round white collar, and a silver watch fob between the pockets of his matching vest indicated that he was no ordinary emigrant. He was leading two horses, a Paint with splotches of brown and white and a smaller horse the color of nutmeg that was carrying packs of supplies.

"Afternoon, Miss." The man's long dark sideburns moved with his angular jaw when he spoke. "Might you be a Winfield?"

Kate's initial alarm subsided. The stranger seemed calm amidst the noisy surroundings. "My name is Dr. Marcus Whitman," he said with a thin smile, doffing the dusty black hat. "I'm looking for the Winfield camp."

Whitman? Where had Kate heard that name?

"I'm Kate Winfield, Mr. Whitman. It appears you've found the right place."

"At last." The gentleman heaved a sigh. "For the whole day I've been riding from company to company looking for you. There are many wagons in this train!" Whitman's bright penetrating eyes were merry. "I'm certainly glad to meet you."

Kate's brain raced. When had she heard his name?

"Would your folks be nearby?" the man asked, giving his Paint more lead.

"Yes, sir. They're over there on the other side of the wagon. Papa's the one in the brown shirt, setting up our tent. The one helping is Joe."

"Thank you, Miss." With his hat back on his head, the stranger led his two horses around the wagon's tongue.

"Dr. Whitman!" Jacob stood up to meet him. "So glad to see you again, sir."

Kate led Midnight closer to the wagon, so she could hear.

"Good to see you again, too, Jacob. This is Joe, I presume?"

Joe politely stood and bowed his white head. "Nice to meet ya, suh," he said.

"And Abby?"

"Abby, come meet Dr. Whitman. Remember? I told you about him. He'll be riding with us for awhile. He's going to lead us past Fort Hall when Gantt leaves."

Then Kate remembered. Papa had met Dr. Whitman in Independence. This stranger was the man who already lived in the Territory and believed they could make it all the way across the mountains, even with this number of wagons and this large a herd.

"Doctor," Abby dusted the flour off her hands. "I've heard about your work with the Cayuse Indians. Won't you stay and have supper with us?"

"That'd be mighty nice, Ma'am. A home-cooked meal for a wandering husband is like a soothing ointment."

After dinner that night, their wagon company seemed at peace in spite of the flurry of its activity. A distant banjo and the sounds of people's voices, laughing and singing, wafted on the breeze. Papa leaned his cane chair back against the big wagon, while Mama sat in her rocker and repaired the torn knees of Jake's breeches with needle and thread. While she stroked Scout behind the ears, Kate could smell the pipe tobacco that Joe was contentedly smoking by the supply wagon. Jake absently whittled on a stick with his penknife, trying to carve something yet to be determined.

By the light of the fire, Dr. Whitman told his story.

"I've been in Boston meeting with the American Board of Commissioners of Foreign Missions." The doctor seemed at ease, resting his elbows on his legs. "They agreed to keep our mission at Walla Walla open, so I'm on my way back home with the good news."

"Doctor," Papa said, shifting a long straw to the other side of his mouth, "if I'm remembering right, you and your wife are the first missionaries in those parts."

"That we are. Along with the Spaldings, who're with the Nez Perce down the Columbia a bit."

"Have you been out there long?" Abby asked.

"Since '36."

As the doctor related their missionary work among the Indians, Kate's heart began to stir. There, sitting in the straight back chair right in front of her eyes, was what she wanted to be—a doctor. Only this man was more. He was a missionary *and* a doctor at the same time. And his wife, a woman, was helping him.

If God was doing it for them, she wondered, might He do it for her, too?

20

BUFFALO!

Friday, June 23

For weeks the emigrants had used timber for firewood, wherever they could find it. Along the Little Blue they had collected plenty of driftwood and had brought enough for several cooking fires after they had left the river. But, on the treeless plains of the Platte River valley, they were forced to turn to a new kind of fuel.

"There's lots of it, almost everywhere ye look. And it burns well." Arkansas's spotted Appaloosa kept shaking his muzzle and mane, itching to run. "I can show ye where to find it."

A band of thin gray light glowed on the eastern horizon. The bugle had already sounded, and someone's rooster greeted the soon-coming dawn. Kate was hungry for a warm breakfast of johnnycakes or what was left of their last bacon slab. She was tired of cold beans and dried beef.

"What is this fuel?" Jacob wondered aloud as he pulled one of the tent's iron stakes from the ground.

"French trappers called it *bois de vache*. Some people call it 'meadow muffins.'"

Wrinkles around the old man's wizened eyes alerted Kate to the fact something might be up. Did she detect the hint of a smile under that thick beard of his?

"What's a meadow muffin?" Jake asked, tugging his left boot on under his pants leg.

"You'll see," was the mountain man's answer. Turning in his saddle to speak to Jacob, he added, "You and Joe might want to hold off hitchin' up yer team. I has a feelin' the train might delay leavin' today. Let me take yer women and Jake out to the field. And ladies, bring some sacks. Ye gonna need 'em."

Arkansas was hiding something, and Kate knew it. Why the mystery? Why wouldn't he tell them what the fuel was?

As it turned out, Abby, Kate and Jake weren't the only ones Arkansas was leading out toward the open range this morning. From the looks of it, every woman and youngster from both the Cow and Light Columns were coming. Kate recognized Mrs. Stevenson and Mrs. Hembree, as well as Mrs. Lenox and Mrs. Campbell. Even Mrs. Eyers had joined in. Once colorful gingham sunbonnets of powder blues and lime greens dotted the landscape like dabs of paint on an artist's canvas. The ladies in their dingy white collared dresses, tattered from miles of wear, walked beside their children—dirty girls in pinafore dresses and grimy boys in patched knickers—everyone anxious to discover this mysterious source of fuel.

For the rest of her life Kate would never forget the shock of what they found out on the plain that day.

Buffalo dung.

Piles of buffalo droppings covered the terrain like large gray-black warts. They were foul, fly infested, and fungus covered. Nauseating. Repulsive.

Lying right at their feet.

"This is it?" Kate moaned, her face contorted. "We have to pick up these?"

"With our bare hands?" Jake wrinkled his nose.

"Looks that way," Abby swallowed hard, and swatted at a fly in front of her face. "Arkansas says it burns. It's all we got."

"Look for the ones that're old enough not to be wet and stinky but fresh enough to make a fire," Betsy Applegate suggested, handing her boys an empty cloth bag. Her flax apron pocket was large enough to hold at least two, so she dropped two in.

Watching the ladies' reactions from horseback, Arkansas chuckled. "You'll get used to 'em, ladies, and even like 'em after a bit. They burn like charcoal but don't smell, and don't smoke much."

"This is dreadful." Jane gingerly selected a small one with her thumb and forefinger. With her arm extended as far as it would go, she plopped it into her bag. "My children will never believe this."

"I don't believe this." Kate bunched the hem of her skirt up above her ankles so it wouldn't touch any of them. "My hands will never be the same."

"Nor my nose," Jane replied, carefully sidestepping a fresh deposit swarming with worms.

"Say, let's start a pile together." Jake's suggestion fell on deaf ears except for Warren and Elisha.

"We'll start here!" Warren announced, planting his boot on top of a large dropping.

Before long, the boys' pile had risen above knee level. "Don't let anyone steal 'em," Kate heard Elisha order like a military officer. "This is our pile."

Within minutes, however, an enemy invasion was detected. One of the boys from the Light Column strolled toward their pile whistling softly. With sun-bleached hair and freckles and breeches rolled up to his ankles, the boy looked like he was a little older than Jake. All of a sudden, the thief grabbed a particularly big chip from their stash and dashed away, in Jake's direction.

"Get him!" Warren yelled.

The twins dashed after the looter, bent on pummeling him to the ground. Jake, however, made use of the ammunition at hand. Selecting a hard chip, he drew back his arm and hurled it toward his target. Whoosh! The chip flew past Kate and whacked the intruder on the cheek. Within seconds, a brown stream was trickling down his face.

"That'll teach ya!" Jake yelled in laughter.

"Jake!" Mama's loud voice thundered across the field. "You get over here this instant!"

Just then, a gust of wind whisked Kate's wavy hair away from her face, and she wished she had remembered her bonnet. The sun was climbing well above the horizon now.

"Jane," Kate started. "Do you feel anything?"

"No," Jane replied. "Just the wind."

"Something's rumbling." Kate tensed. "It almost feels like the ground's moving."

No sooner had the words come out of her mouth than a gigantic cloud of dust arose on the wide-open slope in front of them, filling the western sky. A roar of unending thunder in the distance grew louder and louder. Yet there wasn't a cloud in sight. The ground began to tremble.

Kate could feel her heart pumping. What was happening? Every muscle in her body grew tense.

Then, before Kate's eyes, a great black wooly blur suddenly erupted out of the dust on the horizon.

Buffalo!

Stampeding buffalo!

Kate's feet were frozen to the earth, which was now shaking with the sheer magnitude and force of the charging bison. Galloping at top speed, an army of massive bodies was charging straight at her and the others, the sound of their hooves exploding around them. The air was thick with the smell of wildness. Propelled by some unseen force, the animals came closer and closer, heaving and lunging, the horns on their huge heads thrusting forward in a wall of death.

If Kate had screamed, no one would have heard her. No one heard anything but the stampede.

The buffalo were almost upon them when out of the corner of her eye Kate caught something moving, coming from behind them. Suddenly, amidst the overwhelming thunder of the buffalo, she heard the sharp crack of pistol and rifle shots, then frenzied whooping and hollering and yelling. It was their men! Abby hastily snatched Jake to her side as Jacob and the other hard-riding fathers exploded right through their midst toward the herd, their horses in a flat-out gallop. Pounding straight at the onrushing buffalo, the men fired as they rode.

Kate held her breath. The stampede was only a few hundred feet from the men now! Just as it seemed as if the men would be crushed, several of the leading buffalo stumbled and went down. Slowly at first, and then with growing quickness the stampeding animals began to turn, until finally the entire herd was moving away from them.

As many of the women dropped to their knees, sobbing in relief, Kate watched the men continue their headlong pursuit of the herd that had almost trampled their families. Racing their horses alongside the huge animals, the men tried to fire their weapons into a spot just behind the buffalo's shoulder. When they were successful, the mortally wounded bison would stop running, stagger on for a few more yards, and then collapse on its side in a great dusty heap, dead.

The hunt turned out to be quite successful, because later Kate could see dozens of buffalo carcasses being butchered, which made for very good eating that night.

21

THE SPOILS OF THE HUNT

Friday, June 23

What a hunt it was, John," Jacob replied, licking the leftover juice from his fingers. "This is the sweetest meat I've ever tasted."

"I'll never forget it, that's for sure," Prentiss said as he sopped up some flour gravy with a biscuit. "It seems that we turned them just in time. The ground was black with them."

The smell of fresh roasting buffalo meat created almost a party atmosphere at the campsites tonight. Kate could hear the music of banjos and fiddles, and even a wooden flute. People were dancing and enjoying themselves.

"The best part is the hump rib." Marcus Whitman took another chunk of meat off the skewer and plopped back down on the grass. "Really tender meat. And I must say, Abby, this trail bread is delicious."

"Scout likes it, too," Jake added, throwing the eager dog another bone off his plate. "Joe, do you like it?"

"Tastes like beef to me, Mr. Jake," Joe replied. "A mite gamey but mighty fine."

While everyone else enjoyed the buffalo meat, Kate had to admit that she didn't really like the taste of it all that much, although anything would have been better than more beans and dried beef. Tonight, though, unlike the others, Kate didn't really feel like celebrating. She was still getting over the fright of what had almost happened to them this morning, but she was thinking about something else.

Later that evening she had a chance to go off by herself while the men played cards and the women talked. Kate strolled away from the wagons back toward the field of buffalo dung. A few stars twinkled their presence above her. The deepening golden hues of dusk softened the hills in the west.

Kate stepped around some droppings that had been left. How calm it was this evening. How different from the frightening events of the morning.

Thinking about how close they had come to being trampled, she realized that she was feeling sad. It wasn't that she wasn't grateful for being rescued. She was.

But she was also feeling sad for the animals. Kate couldn't get the dying buffalo out of her mind.

Just then, the sound of a familiar whistling floated through the evening air. Kate would recognize that whistle anywhere. It was Ole Joe.

"Why, Miz Kate, I didn't know you was out here." Joe stopped in front of her and placed both hands on the handle of his wisdom stick, as if he was waiting on something. "I jes' thought I'd take me a short walk."

"Me, too, Joe," Kate replied, tracing a half circle in the sand with the heel of her boot.

"Right purty night," Joe commented, puffing a blue cloud of tobacco smoke from his pipe.

"I guess," Kate sighed.

"Would ya like to talk, Missy?" Joe's question wasn't pushy or overbearing. It was Joe. He had a way of knowing when things were going on inside someone's head. "I brung my wisdom stick, in case I needs it," he smiled.

"I don't know, Joe," Kate began. "Everyone was so happy tonight, and I didn't want to spoil the party. But I can't stop thinking about those poor animals. I think some of the men killed many more buffalo than they needed for food—they were killing them just for the fun of it."

"They did, Missy. That's a fact." Joe's big hand rubbed the knobs on his stick.

"Isn't it wrong, Joe? Isn't it wrong to kill just for sport?"

Joe removed the corncob pipe from his mouth and gazed thoughtfully up toward the smattering of stars. Kate could hear the call of a whooping crane along the distant river bank.

"The Lord gave us dominion over the earth, Missy," Joe finally said. "But I don't think He's real pleased with some of the ways we's handlin' things."

"I know," Kate sighed. "It's one thing to butcher an animal for food, but it's something else to kill it just to prove you can shoot. They left whole carcasses over there for the buzzards. If they keep this up, what will happen?"

Night was descending in its own slow rhythm tonight on the prairie, the crickets and frogs near the river ushering it in.

"I don't know, Miz Kate." Joe drew on his pipe. "Seems like man has a way of destroyin' good at times, both with animals and people, too."

23

SLEEPY GROVE

Friday, June 30

The buffalo hunting continued through the week. Eager hunters from various camps set out to secure fresh meat for the Company, either behind the wagon train or ahead of it. Sometimes they even found buffalo among the cattle, grazing contentedly on the curly bunches of buffalo grass. Other times, as the water holes dried up, an entire herd would migrate toward the river, and the hunters would discover them there. Papa joined the hunt enthusiastically, and so did John Prentiss. With the abundance of meat, Abby created new recipes: buffalo stew, buffalo pie, buffalo jerky, fried buffalo, boiled buffalo tongue, and buffalo soup. Much as she hated to see the animals killed, Kate helped with the cooking.

During the past week the wagons had arrived at the fork of the North and South Platte, and then had proceeded along the south bank of the South Platte while John Gantt searched for a suitable place to ford. The long summer days were scorching and exhausted both the emigrants and their animals. Many of the men were growing increasingly concerned about their animals—especially the oxen, which were pulling thousands of pounds of weight.

Papa was no exception. Just last night Papa had told the family that the Stewarts had already lost one ox and the Applegates were worried about one of theirs. This answered Kate's question about Betsy Applegate's heavy iron cook stove that she had seen abandoned along the trail a couple of days ago. Jacob had also heard that Peter Burnett had been forced to kill one of his oxen, because it just couldn't go any further. "He was just plum worn out," Papa had said. For the past week their oldest ox, eleven-year-old Joshua, had lowered his big old head most of the time—a bad sign.

"We're going to have to think about dumping some weight, Abby, or we'll lose him," Papa had told his wife.

Yesterday John Gantt had sent word that he hadn't found a spot shallow enough to ford the river, so the emigrants would camp that night about eighty-five miles west of the fork and proceed to ferry their animals and belongings across. With so many wagons, Papa said this process would probably take five or six days.

The place was called Sleepy Grove.

Early on Friday morning, as the light trickled through the green diamond-shaped leaves of the cottonwood trees, Kate strolled down toward the river with Jake and Scout to fetch water. The sounds of small morning birds and a barred owl, hidden from view by the big leaves, evoked memories of their farm in Missouri.

Home. It seemed thousands of miles and many years away, even though they had only been traveling for six weeks. It felt like they would never get to Oregon. Their bacon was almost gone, and they were running low on cornmeal. In addition, Kate was worried about Joshua. She had grown up with him. She almost couldn't remember a time when they didn't have the big old ox.

"The mosquitoes are awful bad," Jake complained, breaking into her thoughts.

"Jane told me that buffalo chips keep away the mosquitoes," Kate responded. She smacked a mosquito on her forehead and tugged the brim of her bonnet closer for protection.

"It's bad enough having to pick up the chips and cook with them," Kate went on. "But I can't imagine wiping them all over your skin." At this point she was sorry she hadn't loaded up with some of Mama's catnip oil before they left because it repelled pesky insects like these.

She and Jake followed Scout's wagging tail, growing dirtier by the day, toward the river.

Unlike the beginning of their trip, the Company, both Cow and Light Columns, weren't traveling as columns much anymore. They were more scattered now, moving along in smaller friendly groups, or "marching platoons" as Papa called them, and camping in many smaller corrals instead of just a few large ones. Ole Joe had told her the wagons would probably bunch up again when they crossed the South Platte River in a few days. But for now, Kate and Jake were weaving their way through some of these smaller groups in the midst of the cottonwood grove. Scout scampered ahead out of sight.

Just then, the wind picked up and brought the sound of a low groaning mixed with the whisper of the rustling leaves. The sound was coming from the far side of two wagons and some tents on their right. A dark gold Palomino, tethered to a stake nearby, was quietly munching grass in the morning shade, its tail busily flicking off insects.

"Jake, I think I'll see what's going on," Kate suggested. "That man doesn't sound good."

Two large canvas tents with poles in the center had been pitched near the wagons. Hanging between two trees was a long hemp rope with four damp wrinkled broadcloth shirts flung over it. An iron skillet with crusts of burned food and a dirty fork had been placed on a tree stump. Parked near the ashes of last night's fire were four unwashed tin plates piled high with remnants of buffalo meat. A second smaller fire, built inside a narrow trench, was warming a coffee kettle perched on logs.

And there was the source of the moaning. Curled up on top of a thick velveteen bedroll was a man with curly red hair.

As Kate approached, the flap to one of the tents folded back and a bald headed man with a curly mustache emerged. "Johnson," he scowled. "Did you get any sleep?"

"Not much, Atkins," the man whimpered. "My stomach's tied up in knots."

It was then Kate realized that this was the Easterners' campsite. This was Jeremiah Atkins. And that sick man on the ground must be Lancefield Johnson.

"Ah, I see we have some visitors this morning." Atkins quickly stuffed his bleached muslin shirttail into his striped trousers. "To what do we owe this pleasure, Ma'am?"

There was something about this man Kate didn't like. She couldn't tell whether it was the look in his eyes or the tone of his voice. But she gripped her water bucket with one hand, while she placed her other hand on her brother's shoulder, a sign that she would do the talking.

"Mr. Atkins, I'm Kate Winfield and this is my brother, Jake. We were just passing by."

"The famous Miss Winfield! How do you do?" Atkins twisted the tips of his moustache, trying to curl them even more. "So glad to make your acquaintance at last. I've heard a lot about you."

That fact made Kate feel more uncomfortable. Had John been talking about her? And why?

"What can we do for you?" Atkins asked.

Right then, the pronounced stench of damp dog hair announced Scout's arrival. The dog bounded over to Kate and her brother, stopping to shake off sprays of water.

"Atkins, guess whose dog I met down at—" John Prentiss halted abruptly, right in front of a wagon tongue. "Hello, Miss Winfield," he said, his voice full of surprise. "And Jake! How nice to see you both so early on this beautiful morning." John's deep green shirt set off the green of his eyes. Kate wondered why she had not noticed this before.

"Scout here met me down at the river," John went on, stepping into the campsite. "I was hoping he wasn't lost."

"Not lost, Prentiss," Atkins interjected, clearly not one to be left out of any conversation. "Miss Winfield and her brother were following the dog down to the river when they heard Johnson here."

Kate's level of discomfort was rising. "We were concerned about Mr. Johnson."

"Johnson?" Atkin's laugh carried like a hyena. "He's just been indulging in the finer parts of life on the prairie, you might say." He pulled off the lid to the coffee kettle and poured the hot liquid into a cobalt blue stoneware mug.

"You mean he ate too much buffalo and he's sick?" Jake couldn't be held down any longer. He whacked at a mosquito buzzing his ear.

"Right you are, young man," Atkins replied. "Too much buffalo for him. But not for me! I figure to make up a meat diet and sell it to everybody as soon as I get to Oregon. I'm going to make a fortune on this here buffalo."

It was then Kate realized she really didn't like this man at all. She whirled around to face John.

"Mr. Prentiss, Mama and I have some peppermint back at the wagon. It will soothe Mr. Johnson's stomach. If you'd like to stop by later, I'll give you some."

With that, she grabbed Jake by the shirtsleeve. "Come on, Jake," she ordered. "We've got to get the water."

24

BULL BOATS

Friday, June 30

By late that afternoon, John Prentiss still had not come. But Kate had actually given little thought to him, because Dr. Whitman was telling her how useful the buffalo hides would be in their river crossing.

"The Indians don't waste any of the parts of a buffalo," he related, a bulky buffalo hide folded next to his boots. "I've seen them use the hides for robes, of course, but also the horns for spoons, the intestines for cords, the hair for rope and the stomachs for cooking pots."

"Papa says we're gonna use the hides from bulls to make 'bull boats,' Kate," Jake interjected proudly, straining to hold up a heavy hide.

"The idea is really quite simple," Dr. Whitman offered. "We'll build two boats out of these hides. I've seen it done before."

Kate could easily make out the form of a third buffalo from the black and brown hide Joe was displaying, while a fourth lay jumbled at his feet.

"Can't we get across like we did before, by waterproofing the wagons again?" Kate asked, right before jumping off the wagon's backboard with Mama's sewing box tucked safely under one arm.

"The river's too deep here for the teams to pull the wagons across. And they sure can't swim them across with the wagons loaded. These skin boats will let us ferry our belongings across here, while the teams haul the empty wagon frames over upriver a bit, where it's shallower," Papa explained.

"Miz Kate, we needs you and your Mama to sew two of these together fer each boat," Joe explained, holding up one of the massive skins.

"Mama's checking on Mrs. Stewart right now, Joe. Her baby's coming soon," Kate replied, plopping down in Abby's rocker. "I'll be doing this myself."

She opened the fabric cover of Mama's sewing box. She searched among the wood buttons, the beeswax, and the scissors until she found the needle book and the various threads. Kate picked out the large steel carpet needle, rubbed it along her temple to oil it before sewing, and selected the heavy black cotton thread. It would do nicely for this.

"Joe?" Kate moistened the tip of the thread before slipping it through the eye of the needle. "Did we have to kill more buffalo for these hides?"

Joe's eyes were soft with his smile. "No, Miz Kate. We's usin' the buffalo we already had."

Kate spent the afternoon sewing the hides together, using straight stitches and back tacking like Mama had taught her to prevent the seams from unraveling. Once this was done, Jake helped her remove both of the wagons' bonnets so Jacob, Joe and Dr. Whitman could completely unload the wagons.

When the wagon beds were empty, the three men detached them from the frames and pulled and tugged the furry skins over them as tightly as they could, with the skin to the outside. Jake fetched Papa's hunting knife so Papa could trim the hides where needed, and then they tied the hides to the beds with sinews from the buffalo carcasses. Next, Kate melted buffalo fat, called tallow, and mixed it with ashes. Kate's father and brother smeared the waterproofing mixture onto the skins and especially into the seams. Then the boats were left in the sun to dry out.

"After these skins dry for several days," Papa explained, "the boats will be ready. Then we'll use them together with other people's boats, and float everyone's supplies across the river."

"Those skins should keep the water out," Whitman added with a nod of satisfaction.

Early that evening, when Kate placed the sewing kit back in the wagon, she remembered John Prentiss and the peppermint.

John had never shown up.

25

CROSSING THE SOUTH PLATTE

Tuesday, July 4

For four days the Winfields had waited for the Cow Company's turn to cross the South Platte. They and other waiting emigrants had spent the time repairing gear, socializing with friends, and doing some desperately needed washing.

One morning after breakfast, Kate and her Mama trudged back toward the river. The faint sounds of emigrants and animals crossing upriver filtered through the trees as they carried two heavy wooden barrels piled high with filthy clothes. Two croaking sandhill cranes walked ahead of them, as if leading the way through the forest toward the riverbank.

Dumping the dirty laundry on a large patch of grass under a cottonwood tree, Mama filled the two barrels with river water, one for soapy water and one to rinse. The metal washboard was rough, and scrubbing the clothes in the harsh lye soap they had made back home made Kate's hands sting and turn red. After the clean clothes were rinsed and wrung out, they lugged them back to the campsite and hung everything out to dry. The process took an entire day.

On the Fourth of July, the Winfields' time to cross the South Platte finally arrived. Other families had also made skin boats out of their wagon beds, and these had been added to the Winfields' two boats and brought down to the river to ferry across the Company's goods. The Company's officers had chosen this spot for the operation. Although the river current was faster here than upriver where the teams and empty wagons were crossing, the river was narrower so the crossing would be faster.

For the last several days Kate and Jake had watched as family after family had brought their belongings down to the riverbank and transferred them into the skin boats. A large group of men who could swim were assembled on the south bank, and out of this group six men were assigned to each boat. Some waded and swam alongside the boats, pushing and guiding them, while others pulled by ropes attached to the front.

Papa and Ole Joe and Dr. Whitman had already made several trips across the river helping other families; now it was their turn to take their own goods across. Kate and Mama and Jake helped the men load all of their earthly belongings into the two wagon beds and then ease the skin boats into the shallow water by the bank. She noticed her mother patting her deep apron pocket, which held their precious gourd of seeds.

"No noonin' for us today!" offered Mr. Newby, one of the men helping the Winfields. "I've already made three trips across this blamed river today, and like to make three or four more 'afore we get to sundown."

"Well, we shore do appreciate your help," Jacob responded. "We're all helpin' each other, and we haven't dumped anybody's things in the river yet. Let's hope our luck holds." Kate and Mama exchanged a quick glance and simultaneously said, "Amen!"

Jacob quickly tied ropes to the front of each skin boat, and the six-man crews began to move the boats out into the river. Papa and Joe manned the rope on the large wagon-bed boat while four other men helped, and Dr. Whitman and five helpers were on the supply wagon boat. As the water came up to his waist, Papa called back over his shoulder, "As soon as we get our things across, we'll come back and take you and the teams upriver to cross the wagons up there."

Kate breathed a silent prayer for God to watch over the crossing and keep their things safe.

As the skin boats moved out into the middle of the river, the current began pushing them downriver, forming little waves on the upstream sides of the boats. But the men were able to keep the skin boats from drifting with the current. Once or twice Kate held her breath when one of the men stumbled into a hole in the riverbed and momentarily went under water, losing his hold on the boat. Thankfully the others held steady, and the boats didn't tip.

Kate and Mama both let out huge sighs of relief when the men finally brought their things to the other shore without mishap.

It was at least an hour before the men came back across the river, leaving the Winfields' skin-covered wagon beds to be used by other families. As Papa came out of the river, soaking wet, he explained to Kate that they would pick them up later on the far side, after getting their teams and wagons across.

When they reached the upper river crossing, the scene was one of controlled chaos. The South Platte was about a mile wide at this point and mostly shallow enough to wade across, though there were some deeper holes. The entire distance was filled with shouting men, bawling cattle and nervous horses, teams of lowing oxen, and wagons—sometimes rolling on the river bottom, sometimes floating.

"Papa, look what's happening!" Kate shouted to her father. Many of the emigrants had roped their teams and wagons together in long chains, with groups of men hauling on long ropes from the front. As Kate watched, the front of the column was gradually being pulled further and further downstream by the current, with the result that the rest of the teams and wagons, tied as they were to the column, could only follow helplessly as they missed the opposite landing by more than two miles!

Jacob conferred with Dr. Whitman and Joe, and they decided not to join one of those columns, but to take their chances by roping together just their two wagons. After the yoke of the supply wagon's oxen was securely tied to the back of the larger wagon with a double length of rope, Jacob turned to Kate.

"Let's get moving," he said. "I'll take Mama with me on the big wagon seat, and Joe can take you beside him in the supply wagon. Dr. Whitman has offered to ride Midnight across, pulling Tess, and let Jake ride behind him."

The front seat of the wagon creaked when Papa flicked the reins on Joshua and Caleb's backs and urged them forward. As Balaam and Balak felt the water rise up their legs, they began to groan. "Don't worry, boys," Kate could hear Papa reassure them, "you'll be fine."

As the teams moved further into the river, the water level rose up over the hubs of the wagon wheels. Kate could hear Jake yell "yahoo!" from his spot behind Dr. Whitman, but she was getting worried. How much deeper would it get? The oxen were now exerting extra effort, having to work against the weight of the water and the current, which was splashing merrily against the wagons.

Now the river rose up to the tops of the wheels! Kate turned in her seat to see Midnight bobbing his head up and down and snorting, as the water came up to the bottom of his saddle blanket. In the rear, Tess was groaning her disapproval.

As they neared the middle of the river, they came to a channel where the current was a bit stronger. Papa "hawed" his team to the left against the current, to avoid being pulled downstream, and Joe did the same with the supply wagon.

Suddenly Prudence and Patience stumbled and sank up to their horns. A second later they jerked their heads up and out of the water, gasping for air. They couldn't touch bottom—they were swimming! At that same instant Kate felt the supply wagon begin to float. Both team and wagon began to drift downstream, pulling against the rope tied to Papa's wagon and forcing Midnight and Bessie to follow. "Joe!" Kate cried, gripping the seat for support. "Do something!"

"I'm prayin', Miz Kate, but it'll be all right. Prudence and Patience 'jes hit a hole."

Sure enough, in a few seconds the oxen regained their footing, and as Kate felt the wagon's wheels land back on the river bottom she let out an audible sigh of relief.

The rest of the crossing was uneventful, except that a man on horseback several hundred yards away waved his hat at her. She recognized John Prentiss and his big Palomino horse.

Soon the water began to recede down the wagon wheels as they neared the opposite shore. When the oxen pulled the wagons up onto the river bank, Kate breathed a silent "thank you." They had made it!

Their prayers, and the prayers of others, had worked. Throughout the entire day, not a wagon or animal was lost. The only thing that happened was a few broken axles, but they could be replaced. Joe called the crossing "a miracle."

26

THE GLORIOUS FOURTH

Tuesday, July 4

That evening, after they had put the wagon beds back on the wagons and repacked all their belongings, Mama reminded everybody it was Independence Day. "We're going to celebrate, not just the holiday but our safe crossing!" she announced, hands on her hips just in case anyone might choose to argue.

Of course, no one did.

Before long, a number of other families had joined them.

Their makeshift table had been covered with Abby's only flowered linen tablecloth. Kate had found some wildflowers of blues and yellows that she arranged in a pewter candleholder. Three tallow candles provided light for the gathering.

Catherine Stevenson's platter of freshly baked trail bread was still warm under its checkered cover. The aroma of Betsy Applegate's roast antelope arrived almost before she and her family did. Cynthia Mills, Jane's mother, offered an enormous bowl of steaming baked beans along with her daughter's spicy buffalo jerky. Mama's pickled beets were a special treat for everyone except Jake, who couldn't stand "those purple balls." The biggest success was Kate's plum pudding, saved up especially for the occasion.

Lindsey Applegate swallowed his last spoonful of the pudding. "Why, Miss Kate, this is the best I ever had. It'll make a husband mighty pleased one day." He handed his plate to her, as Kate blushed.

"Thank you, Mr. Applegate," Kate replied, noticing the newly sewn hide patches on the man's elbows.

"I quite agree," chimed in Dr. Whitman, patting his stomach contentedly. "Delicious."

While the women cleared the table, Abby talked about Mrs. Stewart's new baby girl. "It was one of the easiest births I've seen in awhile," she commented, her hands in a bucket of cleaning water. "Outside. On a blanket. Only took two hours."

"That little one let out a wail the moment she was born," Kate added, her fingers greasy from picking up the meat plates. "And she had a head full of black hair."

"Just goes to show you how strong we womenfolk can be!" Catherine surmised as she grabbed the last dish from the table. "Imagine, birthing a baby in the middle of nowhere!"

Kate also snatched a moment with Jane as she folded the tablecloth and set it on the top of Grandpa Winfield's desk, right outside their wagon. "How's it going with William?" she asked.

Jane's beautiful straight teeth showed through her big smile. "Like a dream," she replied. "Last night we danced together for the first time. We've been walking most every night."

As the women worked, the men congregated in a small circle near the Winfields' big wagon. The hooting of a nearby owl in the cottonwoods punctuated the men's conversation. Their words carried easily through the soft night breeze.

"People are edgy, losing their tempers," Lindsey Applegate reported. "Two men argued yesterday back at the grove over which one should fetch some stray cattle. Came to blows, I was told. Some folks are complaining about having to wait for the rest to cross the river. I can see why Burnett quit."

"Gantt says we'll be climbing California Hill day after tomorrow to get over to the North Platte," Ed Stevenson added, dusting off his crumpled hat. "Says it's a pretty long slope. We'll have to watch our animals."

"I'm worried about one of mine." Kate knew Papa was referring to Joshua. "Thinking about unloading a piece of furniture to lighten the load, only it'll break Abby's heart."

At this, Kate's heart sank. She glanced over at Mama, who was carefully piling the washed tin dishes into a pile on the table. How would Mama let go of another precious possession? She had already left so much behind.

"I hear tell we're not far from the driest territory of all." Dillon Mills, Jane's father, whittled while he spoke. "We'll have to be watching our axles, too."

Dr. Whitman fingered his wide wool felt hat as he spoke. "We need to pick up our pace, though. We can't delay any more. People will start to run out of provisions."

He wiped his brow with a grimy kerchief. "You realize, gentlemen, that we're about to make history. A few wagons have reached Walla Walla overland before now, but this is the first large train of wagons. Ever! Once we get there, others will hear about it back east and they'll come. My dream is to see the territory settled, and I'm going to do everything I can to help it happen."

"Hear tell of any more Indian trouble, Whitman?" Lindsey Applegate asked.

The doctor replied. "I don't believe they'll attack us, but some of these tribes can steal a horse faster than a flea can bite a mule."

Right then the strains of Joe's fiddle lit up the night with "Turkey in the Straw." The children scampered over toward him and the mood of the festivities shifted from eating and talking to music and dancing. Mr. Stevenson's banjo and the tapping of Mr. Mills's silver spoons kept the night lively. As the evening came to a close, the entire group gave three cheers to both Uncle Sam and Old Glory.

27

SEEING THE ELEPHANT

Wednesday, July 5

O n Wednesday night Kate tumbled onto her bedroll as the last purples faded from the western horizon. Not even lightning bugs or mosquitoes could keep her from quickly falling into a deep sleep.

It had to have been close to midnight when a distant crack roused Kate's awareness out of her dream state. Had one of the large limbs from a nearby cottonwood rotted and fallen off? Kate's mind easily sank back into sleep. Then, a muted sound, like a lone cow wallowing in the sand to keep cool, began to haunt her. She finally came awake, becoming aware of the night sounds of crickets and frogs.

"Kate, I heard something," Jake broke the stillness.

Mama's voice was prodding Jacob to wake up in their nearby tent.

Around them there was a growing clamor of other voices. Animals began to stir inside the wagons' corral.

Suddenly someone was screaming at the top of his lungs:

"Dr. Whitman! Dr. Whitman! Douglas Osborne shot himself!"

Quickly people began running to the Easterners' camp. As Kate and her family arrived they beheld a ghostly scene. Candles and tar torches that had been lit in haste pushed the blackness of night back into the surrounding trees, showing men and women standing in a circle, many wearing stocking caps and knee-length nightshirts. They spoke in hushed whispers. A lingering odor of gunpowder hung over the site.

Near the glowing ashes of an earlier fire lay Douglas Osborne. His head rested on a down pillow, and a velveteen bedroll, stained with pools of blood, supported his still body. Jeremiah Atkins slumped on a tree stump, his head in his hands, while Lancefield Johnson stood next to him. John

Prentiss covered Osborne with a light gray blanket, but as Kate watched it soon began to turn crimson.

Dr. Whitman picked Abby and Kate out of the watching crowd. "Abby, Kate, I need your help," the doctor began, trying to catch his breath. Folding back the blanket to look at his patient, he said quietly, "This doesn't look good."

Kate jumped forward, ready to do anything she could.

"Kate, heat some water for tea. We'll try to make him comfortable. Abby, I'll need you to make the bandages."

Kate spotted an iron kettle.

"I'll get it," John offered. "Jake, fetch me that water bucket over there."

The crowd grew deathly quiet while the doctor examined the wounded man, now moaning with every breath.

"He's shot himself in the stomach," Whitman finally announced. The sadness in his voice was evident. "The shot has penetrated his abdomen, shattered his right ribs, and gone through his back. The only thing I can do is to make him comfortable."

The murmuring sounds around Kate indicated that the crowd had quickly realized what Dr. Whitman was saying. Douglas Osborne was dying. Her heart sank.

"You folks need to go on back to your camps," Whitman ordered, standing to his feet and wiping the blood off both hands with the handkerchief out of his back pocket. "There's nothing you can do now but pray." Then under his breath he added, "There's nothing any of us can do but pray."

Slowly the throng of emigrants ebbed back to their individual tents. An almost tangible sadness filled the air. The 1843 Oregon Emigrating Company had witnessed a terrible accident, a tragedy it would never forget.

They had "seen the elephant."

"How did this happen?" Kate asked John as she put more sticks on the small fire under an iron grate. The kettle sitting on the grate was beginning to steam.

"He couldn't sleep," John replied. "I think he was excited about tomorrow, because he was to be one of the buffalo hunters going ahead of the train."

"What was he shooting in the middle of the night?" Kate dusted her hands on her linen jacket, glad she had worn it over her nightgown.

"He was cleaning his gun."

"In the dark?"

"By the light of the fire."

While the water boiled, Kate watched Dr. Whitman and her mother work on the patient. The doctor used tweezers to remove any pieces of Osborne's shirt he could find in the wound. While he was doing this, Abby cut a large piece of white cotton tow cloth for the first bandage and then began tearing long strips for ties. They had stopped most of the flow of blood from the wound, but there was no telling how much Osborne was bleeding internally. His breathing was labored and shallow.

Dr. Whitman's face was pale in the torchlight, but Kate could see on it smears of dried blood. He moved quickly to tie the large bandage around the man's abdomen, the tenderness for his patient reflected in his deep brown eyes. But there was nothing more he could do. Douglas Osborne was in God's hands now.

Just then, Mr. Osborne moaned.

"Kate, we'll have that tea now," Whitman motioned.

Over the next few hours, the family and Osborne's traveling companions held vigil around the dying man. Each person took turns sitting on the ground beside him, holding his clammy hands, thinking and praying. Dr. Whitman's Bible offered the opportunity for people to read aloud to him. For quite a while, the man's blood oozed through the bandages, so Abby and Kate helped the doctor change them.

As the night wore on, Abby suggested to Jacob that Jake was "needing to go on back." The ten-year-old was curled up under the Easterners' wagon, his head nestled near Scout's front paws, who had come with the family. "I must stay," she told her husband as she wound some fresh bandages into a ball. "And Kate should learn."

"This is moving toward doctoring for her." Jacob frowned. "You know my feelings on this, Abby. Doctoring isn't for women."

"Now, Jacob," Abby's eyes were tender toward her husband. "This man hasn't got much longer. We can discuss this later."

Her father's reluctance was clear to Kate as Jake sleepily let his father carry him back to the wagon. If Papa didn't want her staying here tonight, how would he ever agree to the idea of his only daughter becoming a doctor and living far away in some distant land? Her Mama's words to "leave this in God's hands" echoed within her soul. She hoped she would be able to do that.

As the hours moved toward morning, the only sounds were the hauntingly familiar refrains of toads and crickets and an occasional wolf. The wounded man did not regain consciousness.

Until the first hint of dawn. His eyes, glazed and exhausted, slowly opened.

"Kate, quick. More tea!" Abby directed.

Mr. Johnson propped up his friend's head, while Abby dribbled a spoonful of the warm water onto his parched lips. Streams of perspiration from a fever drained down the sides of the man's face. Agony poured from his eyes.

"I know . . . I'm going . . . to die." Osborne stammered. A hacking cough followed most of his words. "I am . . . glad . . . to have . . . known you."

Dr. Whitman interrupted, "Osborne, don't try to talk."

"I . . . have to . . . say something," the man replied with irritation. "And . . . I . . . don't . . . have much . . . time . . . to say it." His head dropped back on the pillow for a moment. Abby offered another spoonful of tea.

Mustering his last strength, he lifted his head and looked at each one of them in turn. "Make . . . your . . . peace." His last words were raspy, struggling to get out with each breath. "With . . . each other . . . and . . . with God."

His head dropped back, and with a long sigh Douglas Osborne departed this life. He was twenty-eight years old.

Dr. Whitman gently closed the man's eyes.

28

LIFE AND DEATH

Thursday, July 6

That morning at the bugle's call to leave, the Winfields and a number of other emigrants remained behind for Osborne's burial service.

John's moss green shirt and slate gray breeches were spattered with dirt when Kate arrived. He and Lancefield had finished digging the grave at a site under some towering cottonwood trees, not far from the South Platte. The hole was six feet deep, so the wolves wouldn't dig up and eat the remains. Covering Mr. Osborne's body was the same velveteen bedroll that Kate had seen under Mr. Johnson a few days ago. The smell of the river mud and the men's sweat permeated the early morning air.

"What about a marker?" John asked Dr. Whitman as he leaned on his shovel.

"We aren't going to leave one," Whitman replied as he opened his Bible. "The Indians will dig him up for his clothes."

No marker? Kate could hardly believe it. How would Mr. Osborne's grave ever be found, if there was no engraved stone or even a wooden cross with his name on it? His family back east would never know where to find it.

The Winfields had put on their best clothes, wrinkled as they were from weeks in the trunk. Papa wore his one jacket, a chestnut frockcoat, and Mama had on her plaid dress with its high waist, scooped bodice and puff sleeves. Jake's black breeches were a bit short on his growing legs, but Kate's tea dress with its yellow lace still fit her well. Even Ole Joe had brought out the black satin vest Bessie had given him not long before she died. The thought crossed Kate's mind that at least they each had one article of clothing left without patches or stains.

Soft cottonwood seeds fluttered down in the wind as Dr. Whitman began the service. "Lord, Thou hast been our dwelling place in all generations . . ." Psalm 90 resonated through the forest.

After a prayer Dr. Whitman offered time for anyone who would like to speak. After Mr. Atkins and Lancefield Johnson said a few words about their friend, John Prentiss stepped forward.

"Douglas was a good man." John's voice wavered as his dark green eyes focused on the cloaked body. "When he and I left Philadelphia, we never dreamed anything like this would happen. His death makes me think about what's really important." John's hands scrunched his felt hat and his eyes scanned the small crowd, finally settling on Kate. "A man had better decide how he wants to spend the rest of life, because he never knows when he'll have to face God."

After the service Kate and her family returned to their wagons to change their clothes, break down their camp, and hitch the teams. Papa said they would catch up with the others and would also meet Dr. Whitman, who was riding ahead.

Kate stumbled numbly through her chores. The laundry she and Mama had labored over yesterday wasn't totally dry, and Tess seemed irritable when Kate milked her. Midnight even nipped at her when she untied his tether.

Questions about life and death swirled through her mind. She wanted to try to figure things out, yet she didn't want to face such awful realities. This was the first death she had ever witnessed, but she had a feeling it wouldn't be the last, even on this wagon train. The reality of how fast life could turn into death had flowed into her mind like a river flooding its banks. And the worst of it was that Kate knew she had to accept the lesson of Osborne's accident: Death was part of life.

"Why, Joe?" The wind carried Kate's question to Joe's ears as she gripped both of Patience's horns. Joe was centering the U-shaped ring of the yoke's crossbar under the ox's neck. "Why did Osborne have to die?"

"I don't know, Missy." The man's dark muscles bulged as he squared the yoke to make it comfortable.

"He had his whole life in front of him."

"Only the good Lord knows our time to go."

"How can a good Lord let such a bad thing happen?" Kate went on.

"Don't know that, neither." The deep lines in Joe's black skin reminded Kate that he had lost his own wife. Then he added, "Watch yer thoughts ther, Missy. Faith grows from readin' God's Word; but we can wreck it with our thoughts. Thinkin' on things we can't figure out can plague us, if we let it, Miz Kate.

Patience stamped a foot. "Besides," Joe went on, "God has a way of bringin' good out of bad. You'll see. Settle it that you'll enjoy today and what the Lord brings our way. Somethin' good will happen, and it'll be because God hears our prayers."

"Ready?" Papa yelled with a determined set in his bearded jaw.

Kate tied her flowered sunbonnet under her chin and whistled to Scout, who scurried up with his tongue hanging and his tail wagging, looking for affection.

It wasn't until that moment that she noticed.

Resting behind them near an ancient cottonwood was Grandpa Winfield's walnut desk. Abandoned and alone.

29

WINDLASS HILL

Thursday, July 6

The day was brutally hot. The wagons slowly crept up the long incline of California Hill, the straining oxen's tongues hanging out for water, though there was none to be had. When they reached the crest, Kate knew they still had more than fifteen miles to go until they came to the North Platte River. With eyes narrowed against the dust and flies, and sweat streaking down their flanks, the Winfields' faithful animals pulled the banging, clattering wagons northwest along a treeless and waterless high plateau under a broiling sun, the family trudging beside them, one step at a time. The ever-present wind brought no relief, for it blew hot and dry air.

At the nooning no one seemed very hungry. People carefully rationed sips of water from their canteens, and Kate gave a ladle of water to each of the oxen, Midnight, Tess, and Scout. Everyone sought the only shade available—under the wagons.

All too soon, the bugle sounded, and the emigrants resumed their slow trek over the plateau.

It was too hot to do anything except to try to keep walking and avoid stepping on the prickly pear cactus spines. The stifling afternoon wore on and on.

Just when Kate was wondering how much more of this heat she could take, they finally reached another hill, on which were gathered wagons and teams. When the Winfields reached the top, they soon discovered why everyone had stopped. On the other side of the crest the hill seemed to end abruptly, dropping almost straight down through ravines to a green and lush valley floor below. As far as Kate could see, the bluff extended for miles to both the right and the left. There was no other way to get to the North Platte River. They had to find a way to get down the ravines.

"Papa, how're we gonna do this?" Jake verbalized the question in Kate's mind as she clutched the hair between Scout's shoulders to stop him from sprinting down the slope on his own.

Jacob stood by his panting team. "The slope has to be a 25-degree drop, Joe, and it's at least three hundred feet to the bottom. I haven't ever seen anything like it. What do you think?" Even Balaam's big old black eyes drooped with apprehension.

Joe rubbed the stubble on his dark chin as if this would help him figure things out. "Might need to think on this one, Mistah Jacob," Joe replied. "I'm wishin' we'd brung our windlass."

Edward Stevenson, whose wagon was parked farther up the ridge, approached, wiping the back of his neck with a dirty kerchief. "Jacob!" he said. "There's got to be a way to do this without losin' everything. Got any ideas?"

"Papa." Kate untied and retied her bonnet and ventured forward. "We can do this. Let's pray and ask God to show us how."

The rustle of her mother's long pinafore behind Kate announced her presence. Abby stamped the afternoon's dust off her boots. "She's right, Jacob," she added. "We need to pray."

Before Papa could respond the unsociable crusty voice of another emigrant intruded on their conversation. "Well, if it isn't the old gang," the man growled. "Thinking about how you're going to get down?"

The creases around Mr. Eyers's lips created a permanent scowl. "Those oxen aren't going anywhere, Winfield. Now, my 'ole mules here? Why, they can get down this here hill in a flash." The man's suspenders snapped when Eyers thumbed them, a sign of his nauseating confidence. "It can't be as hard as it looks."

"How do you propose to do it, Eyers?" Jacob asked, with a hint of disgust.

"I'll just turn this here supply wagon toward the closest ravine and let them have a go!" A long stream of mud colored tobacco juice splattered the sand when Eyers spat. He laughed so loud that he startled some nearby sparrows into flight.

At that point Joe shuffled over toward the man and his mules. "Mr. Eyers, suh," he began in his deep Southern drawl. "I wouldn't do that if'n I was you. I'd try to brake my wagon by lockin' the wheels to the bed with chains." Gesturing toward some small trees growing on the downward slope, he said, "You could also cut down a few of them trees over thar first and stick 'em through the spokes of yer back wheels."

Kate could tell Joe had been "thinking on" the problem.

"Joe's right, Eyers," Jacob chimed in, patting an anxious Caleb on his hind end. "This hill's way too steep. We can tie some ropes on the wheels, too, to hold the wagons back even more."

Eyers spat again, only this time it was in disgust. "No nigger's going to tell me what to do, Winfield. Just you watch now."

The loud baying of Eyers's mules echoed in Kate's ears long after his two animals started forward under their owner's sharp whip. For long seconds she could see the mules frantically scrambling for solid footing amidst the dirt and rocks sliding down into the ravine under their feet. It was as if it were happening in slow motion—the heavy wooden wagon lurching forward way too quickly, slowly turning sideways to slide down the ravine, the loud snap of the wagon's front tongue, and then the cracks of splintering wood as it overturned, sending sacks of flour and cornmeal, a barrel of lard and other supplies careening down the hill. When the smashed wagon stopped rolling, Eyers's two frenzied mules, abruptly freed from their leather leads, jumped and slid the rest of the way down the ravine. They were dazed but not hurt.

And Mr. Eyers? He stood halfway down the hill in the dust scratching his gritty gray sideburns.

"We'd best listen to your man, Jacob," Mr. Stevenson remarked, hiding a grin at Eyers's plight. "I think he's got the right idea."

If they could slow down the speed of descent, they just might be able to do this. The emigrants used small tree trunks placed inside the wheels, as Ole Joe had suggested. Getting out the ropes used to cross the South Platte, they tied the ends to the rear wheels of the wagons, and groups of men standing on the top hauled back on the ropes and played them out slowly, as the oxen carefully worked their way down the ravines.

When it came their turn, Papa and Joe wedged the tree trunks between the spokes of their wagons' back wheels, and with the assistance of Dr. Whitman and other men on the ropes eased both wagons and the teams down the tricky slope. It was hard work, but the only mishap was a broken axle on the Winfields' supply wagon. And Papa and Joe could fashion a new one from a small tree.

Grateful to be safely on the valley floor, Papa looked back over his shoulder at the steep drop they had just navigated and chuckled to Kate, "We should call that place Windlass Hill, 'cause of the windlass we didn't have! Maybe the next trains will bring one."

30

ASH HOLLOW

Friday, July 7

Kate couldn't take her gaze off the beauty before her. A lush grassy meadow, bordered by tall ash trees on the left, led to a lake of clear blue water, fed by springs gushing out of the limestone cliffs on the right. She quickly realized that no one would need to hunt for buffalo chips here—the abundant trees afforded plenty of timber for fires. Wild red roses and wildflowers were a delight to eyes that had lately seen nothing but sand and sagebrush. The cattle, oxen, and horses contentedly grazed in the meadow. As Dr. Whitman had promised them, after the ordeal of what they now called Windlass Hill, this place was a much-needed blessing.

This morning after breakfast everyone had gotten busy. While Papa and Joe had repaired the broken axle, Jake had soaked that same front wheel that was always shrinking in the heat. Kate had mended a tear in the wagon's bonnet and Abby had aired out the bedrolls. Now, while Jake and his trusty cattle herder, Scout, were looking after their cows, Abby and Kate were with some of the other women, gathering wild currants.

"Who would've thought?" Jane Mills declared, picking a cluster of red currants off a vine and popping them into her wooden bucket. "What a discovery!"

"Let's make currant pudding tonight, Mama." The harsh voices of some black crows nearly drowned out Kate's suggestion.

Standing on her toes, Catherine Stevenson stretched up into a bush of plump red berries six feet high and yanked at the fruit. After dropping her find into her metal pail, she paused to catch her breath. "I'm thinking that God Himself has led us beside these quiet waters on His Sabbath, ladies," she offered. "I've been so tired lately. And hot. And dirty. Wondering if

I'll ever be the same. I could settle right here in this canyon and be happy. Sure as a cat naps on a hearth."

"I'm not sure your man would be happy about that," Abby countered, her fingers growing red with the juice. "But this place surely restores a tired soul."

"By the way, has anyone seen Louesa Lenox lately?" Cynthia Mills was arranging her berries so they wouldn't get squished in her wooden bucket. "I heard her girls were sickly."

"All four girls?" Abby replied with concern.

"I believe so," Cynthia replied, picking another bunch of currants.

That day at lunch, Abby mentioned Mrs. Mills's concern to Dr. Whitman.

"It's probably just an upset stomach from all the changes in diet," he commented. "But we'd better have a look."

"Would you mind if Kate went with you, doctor?" Abby eyed her daughter with a smile. "I'd like to get this pudding done by supper."

Situated in the shade of some tall ash trees, the Lenox campsite appeared strangely quiet. The sound of the leaves rustling with scurrying squirrels and the distinctive notes of a black-billed cuckoo should have given the scene a feeling of happiness. But it didn't. Something was wrong.

Only one tent had been set up for the large family. The yellowing cloth covering their supply wagon had yet to be removed. A broken tongue on their prairie schooner was still waiting to be repaired. A plate of dried biscuits on a stump invited black ants.

Where were the toys, Kate wondered? Four children and not a toy in sight. No jump ropes. No pick up sticks. And not one single doll. This didn't make sense.

Just then, the hushed sound of a crying child reached their ears.

"Louesa?" Dr. Whitman inquired. "I came to check on you. Are you here?"

The canvas tent flap rustled and Louesa Lenox emerged through the opening. Dark circles under her eyes and uncombed stringy blonde curls revealed a lack of sleep.

"Hello, Doctor." She tucked some limp curls behind her ears and brushed her wrinkled apron in an attempt to be presentable. "You too, Kate."

"We heard some of your young'uns might be sick," Whitman began. He momentarily deposited his large medical bag, made of stiff brown cowhide, in the sand.

"It's all four girls, Doc. Been feelin' poorly for a couple of days. David's gone to fetch another bucket of water. I'm fit to be tied. Don't know what else to do. I thought after Mary got burned that nothing else would happen to us."

"Can I take a look?" Whitman asked, picking up his bag. "Kate, why don't you come with me?"

A short while later, the two of them emerged from the tent to find two worried parents waiting outside.

"What do you think, Kate?"

Kate was dumbfounded. "You're asking me what I think, sir?" she responded.

"I'd like to know your diagnosis."

Kate swallowed hard. A medical doctor had actually asked her opinion! Well, if he wanted to know, then she would tell him.

"A child's normal temperature is between 96.8 degrees and 99.4 degrees," she began. "The girls' fevers range between 101 degrees and 102 degrees. It's been awfully hot recently, so I'm wondering if these fevers are the result of dehydration."

Kate paused a moment with her hands at her hips. "Since their fevers aren't dangerously high, we don't need licorice root or thyme. At least not yet. I think I'd try catnip or echinacea first and see what happens."

Dr. Whitman turned to the parents, who had been listening. "Kate has made a good diagnosis. I agree with her. Your girls have developed a fever for some reason. The best treatment is to keep them cool and give them this catnip." He rummaged in his bag for the vial. "But you must put the girls in their own tent. I don't want you sleeping with them, Louesa. Sleep close, right outside if you want to, but don't sleep with them. I'll check back tonight to see how they're doing."

On their way back to the Winfields' campsite, Kate asked the doctor why he had insisted that the parents not sleep with the girls, and keep them in a separate tent.

"Sometimes you have to isolate people with fevers, Kate, so no one else gets sick," he replied. "We're not sure why, but it often keeps other people from catching the fever."

Kate made a mental note to remember that.

31

THE CRIMSON CROSS

Friday Evening, July 7

Except for the whippoorwills and crickets and the strains of music from the distant camps, it was quiet at the Winfield site this night. Abby was serenely rocking as she read her Bible by the light of the fire. Jake was happily playing with the Applegate twins, and the familiar aroma of Joe's corn cob pipe hovered over the camp.

Mama looked contented, Kate noted, and she knew why. Papa was satisfied that everything was ready for them to hit the trail tomorrow, and her daughter had been encouraged today in her dream about being a doctor. These things brought contentment to a mother's heart.

Kate tugged a long strand of gray sheep's wool from the skein. Knitting a sweater for Papa had been Mama's idea. "September is cool in the mountains," she had said. "He'll need it." As Kate wrapped the yarn around four fingers several times to begin the ball, she thought again about her mother.

Mama hadn't wanted this trip to Oregon, yet she had never voiced a word of resentment toward Papa about it. Not one. Kate suspected that, given the chance, her mother would return to the farm in a moment. Mama had created a warm and comfortable place back home—a log cabin with ruffled curtains, fresh flowers, and warm cookies. Even at seventeen Kate knew that for a woman to leave all that was heart wrenching.

She also understood that her mother would never cross her father. Not only did Abby love Jacob and respect him, but she believed it was her husband's place to make the decision about where they would live. Kate silently wondered whether Papa truly appreciated how much it had cost Mama to leave Missouri.

Just then Dr. Whitman arrived at the campsite. "The Mills girls still have fevers," he reported as he unbuttoned his high collar. "But, they seem to be doing better. Jacob, I think Kate might have a gift for medicine."

Instantly Kate tensed. The doctor had dared to bring this up to Papa? What would Papa say?

The legs on her father's chair squeaked in the dirt as he shifted his weight. "Yep. Kate does have a heart to help people, doctor. That's a fact."

Whitman continued as if he was thinking out loud. "There'll be plenty of opportunities for her out here on the trail. Why, I can even see her helping us at the mission—"

"Doctor, I don't mean to be rude, but I got strong feelings about this." Papa's large arms crossed his chest. "The first place a woman needs to help is home, and that's what Kate will be doing." His tone signaled the end of the conversation.

Kate didn't understand why Papa was so closed about this. After all, hadn't God created women with gifts, too? Kate knew that women could become nurses, and that was important. But why could only men be doctors?

She wasn't surprised by her father's reaction, but she was very disappointed. Kate didn't doubt that her father loved her, but to him a woman's place was at home, and that was that. Kate's dream could never come true without her Papa's blessing, but how was God going to change the mind of a man who was so set in his ways? Hopelessness flooded Kate's heart. The dream seemed farther away than ever.

Dr. Whitman didn't seem ruffled by Jacob's response. He changed the subject. "By the way, Mrs. Winfield, I came upon Jake on his way to the river with the Applegate twins. Asked me to let you know he's going frog hunting."

"If we wait on him, we might starve, doctor," Abby chuckled as she fingered a silver chain place keeper in the folds of her Bible.

Kate pushed her hopeless feelings away and determined that she wasn't going to dwell on them, at least not now.

A glint from Mama's place keeper caught Kate's eye. Attached to the chain was a thin silver cross, which fit snugly in the creases of Mama's Bible. Kate remembered holding it when Mama would read the Bible to her as a child.

"Mrs. Winfield, that's a beautiful book mark," the doctor commented. "It looks valuable."

"That it is," Abby replied. "But not just because of the silver." The cross reflected the light from the fire. "It belonged to my great aunt, who left it to me when she died."

"I, too, have a cross that is very precious." The doctor's voice seemed far away.

"What kind of cross, Dr. Whitman?" Kate inquired. The ball of yarn Kate was winding was getting bigger.

"A cross with a wonderful story," he began. "A story that goes back for many hundreds of years."

That night, as the shadows lengthened around the Winfield wagons, Dr. Whitman related the legend of the Crimson Cross.

"At the time of the last Crusade, a Spanish knight was praying in a ruined church in Jerusalem, when he discovered in the dust a beautiful cross—about as big as your Bible there," he said, indicating Abby's Bible.

"It was made of finely worked silver filigree, with five large rubies—one at the end of each arm, and one in the center—for the five wounds of Christ. He sailed for Spain with the cross, knowing that it was the most valuable thing he had ever owned.

"But his ship was caught in a terrible storm and began to sink. Crying out to God, he made a vow that if his life was spared, he would give the cross to a Franciscan monastery on the south coast of Spain."

Jakes eyes grew wide. "What happened to him?" he asked eagerly.

Dr. Whitman smiled. "God heard his prayers. The ship did not sink, and the knight made it home safely. He kept his word and gave the cross to the La Rabida monastery, where it stayed until the abbot felt led by God to give it to Christopher Columbus, just before he sailed to the New World in 1492.

"Columbus gave it to his cabin boy, and eventually the cross came to England with the Spanish Armada. I was told that William Bradford brought it to America on the *Mayflower* and gave it to a Pilgrim girl named Mercy Clifton. Many generations later Pastor George Duffield of Philadelphia passed it on to a youth named Nate Donovan. It was later given to a young man who went to the Pacific with Lewis and Clark, and he in turn handed it over to a midshipman on the *U.S.S. Constitution*."

"That midshipman gave it to me, back in '36, before I went to the Oregon Territory for the first time."

"Doctor, what an amazing story!" Abby poked the logs on their dying fire into flame.

"Well, I haven't told you the most important part," said Dr. Whitman, hitching his chair closer to the fire. "When the cross is given to someone, that person must pledge to live a life worthy of the Savior who died upon it for us. And everyone who receives the cross must promise that in their older years, they will pass it on to the person God points out to them—a person who will further His plan for America."

Jacob looked at Dr. Whitman across the fire. "And now you own this cross, Doctor." It was more of a statement than a question.

"Indeed I do, Jacob. I hope that in my own small way I am furthering God's plan for our country by ministering to the Indians of the Oregon Territory and encouraging our people to cross the continent and settle there."

"There is no question about that, Doctor," Abby said with certainty.

Kate tucked the last strand of yarn into the ball and wondered what a young man would have to do to become worthy enough to receive the Crimson Cross.

32

CHIMNEY ROCK

Saturday–Sunday, July 8–9

The tranquil shade and water of Ash Hollow behind them, the emigrants were traveling through a dry and dusty country, with no trees and little vegetation. The tall, lush grasses of the prairie had long since given way to short buffalo grass that grew in sparse clumps.

"I wish we could've stayed at Ash Hollow some more." Jake was walking along next to Patience, absently flicking at her flank with a switch. Patience indicated her annoyance with a snort.

"Oh, stop grumbling, Jake," responded Mama. "At least it's cooler today."

"Yep, cooler than it should be out here for July, I'm thinkin'," said Papa. "And stop bothering Patience, son. She doesn't like it." Jake tossed his switch to Scout, who happily picked it up and walked along with it sideways in his mouth.

"Maybe it's the thunderstorms around," Kate offered to no one in particular, eyeing distant flashes of lightning coming out of dark rain clouds on the other side of the river.

"Joe, that creaking wagon wheel is about driving me plum crazy!" Mama turned around and pointed at the right front wheel of the supply wagon.

"Yes'm," responded Joe from his place beside Joshua and Caleb, who were pulling the supply wagon today. "I'll put the axle grease to it when we stop fer the noonin.'"

The next day, after the nooning, the wagons were rolling northwest, up the valley of the North Platte River. As best they could, they were staying close to the river's southern bank, to keep their water supply nearby.

Kate pulled off her bonnet and used it to slap the trail dust off her freshly washed calico skirt. "I can see why they call this 'The Great American Desert,' Papa," she called to her father. "There's nothing out here but dirt and a little grass!" Stretching ahead as far as they could see was a landscape of brown sand and rock with sparse clumps of short buffalo grass.

"Yep, but it's mostly flat, and that's better for the animals. We can make more miles each day." Papa was always thinking about what was best for the cattle and the oxen.

"Papa, look there! Just like Mr. Gantt said!" Jake was pointing at two enormous rock formations that loomed in front of them, rising starkly from the plain about twenty miles away. At the nooning the pilot had told them that they were coming into an area of the country that contained large sand and rock shapes, unlike anything these farmers and their families had ever seen.

"Why did they name 'em Jailhouse and Courthouse, Papa?" Kate asked, remembering that Mr. Gantt had said that the first two formations they would come to were called Jailhouse Rock and Courthouse Rock.

"Don't know, Kate," her father replied. "Must have reminded somebody of buildings back home, I guess." Kate thought that Jailhouse Rock, now silhouetted against a western sky and turning gold in the late afternoon sun, didn't look much like the jailhouse she had seen in the nearest town back home. But with a little imagination it was easy to think that Courthouse Rock definitely resembled the square courthouse in the county seat. Sitting next to each other, the stark and majestic rock formations jutted into the sky some four hundred feet above the plain.

A few miles farther the Cow Column drew near to another strange rock formation that had first been clearly visible from a distance of about thirty miles—Chimney Rock. From a great circular rock pile, a tall, straight chimney-like spire rose straight up into the air for a distance of at least three hundred feet. In the clear dry air, distances were deceptive, but Jacob and Joe guessed that the base was at least one hundred and fifty feet high, making the whole formation more than four hundred and fifty feet tall!

"Jacob," Abby suddenly called. "What is that Indian doing over there?"

Less than half a mile away, on the top of a small bluff, a lone Indian sat astride a Painted pony, watching the wagons pass. Clad in buckskin leggings, he wore an eagle feather stuck in his long pulled-back black hair.

A buffalo-hide shield was strapped to the arm that held the reins, and in the other he cradled a spear that reflected the late afternoon sun. Neither the Indian nor his pony moved. They were absolutely motionless.

"I don't know, Abby," replied her father. "I think he's just watching us."

Long after they had passed him, Kate saw that he was still there, as if made of the same stone as Chimney Rock. What does he think of us, she wondered. Does he feel that we are invading his land, or is it all right with him that we are just passing through?

"Missy, this is a strange land." Ole Joe shook his head. "Strange rocks, strange Indians. Don't rightly know how to think on it."

Up ahead, as the front of the column reached a spot only several miles from Chimney Rock, Kate could see John Gantt beginning to circle the wagons for the evening.

"It is indeed a strange land, Joe," Kate responded. She knew that Joe would likely spend some time "thinkin' on it."

So would she.

33

SCOTT'S BLUFF

Monday, July 10

As Chimney Rock receded behind the emigrants, the most spectacular rock formation they had yet seen loomed ahead. A high range of sandstone bluffs towered over the plain to their right. Joe said that this was a landscape he wouldn't soon forget because he had "pret'near mem'rized it, what with walkin' toward it and all."

After dinner that evening, John Prentiss rode over to the Winfields' wagons, which were parked in short golden grasses near the bluffs. With him were a number of young people, including William Vaughn and Jane Mills.

"John, it's good to see you again," Abby commented as she tied the drawstring around the top of a burlap sack. Their flour was dwindling fast. "Where are you off to?"

"We're wondering if Kate might be available to walk with us out to the bluffs, Mrs. Winfield," John inquired. "We should be back before dark."

Abby eyed Kate's father, who was fitting a strip of leather into his boot to cover a hole in its sole. "We don't usually let Kate just go off like this, Mr. Prentiss," Jacob replied. "But it seems all right. Kate, would you like to go?"

From the moment John had asked, Kate had hoped to go. "Yes, Papa, I would," she responded, tugging at the bow behind her back and flinging her apron onto the wagon wheel.

"I guess that decides it then," Papa smiled through his beard.

"And don't forget," Abby chimed in. "Arkansas is stopping by later with a tale. In fact, why don't all of you come by and listen."

John helped Kate up behind him on his horse, and the small group of young people rode out through low grasses and sagebrush toward the massive pile of sandstone called Scott's Bluff. It was actually a range of large bronze and rust-colored ledges chiseled by nature out of volcanic eruptions. This evening a mist was settling over the tops of the bluffs, as if quietly announcing the coming of fall.

"Look! Back there!" Jane exclaimed, after they had been climbing up over the ledges for awhile.

Far in the distance behind them, a herd of bison slowly migrated across the flatland, like a giant flow of ink from an inkwell.

"I've been watching for them since I went out on the last hunt," William commented, as he joined Jane's arm in his. "Never seen anything like it."

It was a beautiful land, one that offered numerous opportunities to marvel at God's creation. After a long climb to the top, the young people found themselves on a rocky shelf about eight hundred feet above the valley. The view in the rapidly setting sun was breathtaking. To the south, there were ridges of reddish sandstone rock, and to the north the Platte River valley stretched for as far as they could see. When they heard the high pitched "kree . . . kree . . . kree" of a prairie falcon, whose nest they were near, everyone hushed so they wouldn't scare it away.

"Kate, what do you think this is?" John asked quietly. The rock in his hands was shaped like a dome. Kate's fingers rubbed the distinct bumpy ridges along the top.

"Almost looks like an ancient shell," John mused, handing it to her. "A tortoise maybe?"

"That's what it is, John!" Kate responded. "A petrified turtle shell."

She weighed it in her hand. "Feel how heavy it is. Look, there are more!"

Sure enough, imbedded in the sandstone around them were dozens of the fossils, all shaped like turtle shells, some as much as two feet across. "I imagine that they're thousands of years old," John went on, depositing his relic back on the sand. "Back then they must have been down in the river.

"I wonder how long they lived," asked John. "Everything has to die at some time."

John's words hovered in the breeze for a moment as though they had a greater meaning. Kate sensed that he might want to talk. She picked up a small turtle fossil and slipped it in the pocket of her yellow plaid skirt for a souvenir.

"I'm sure you must miss Mr. Osborne, John," Kate ventured. "He was the first person I've ever watched die. His death was hard for me."

"Me, too," John responded. He looked intently at her. "Before I came on this trip, Kate, I was sure about everything. I had my life mapped out."

The words came out of him in a rush. "I think what I really wanted was the adventure of it. That's why I hooked up with Osborne. He was convinced this would be the trip of all trips." He paused.

"Osborne was right about the trip, but not for the reasons he thought," the young man continued. "I'm not the same as I was when we left. I'm changing." John slowly stood up. "I'm not exactly sure what it all means, but I aim to give myself—and God—time to sort it out."

John's words stayed with Kate as they joined the others and headed back to the Winfields' campsite. The sun was all the way down now, and darkness was rapidly descending. The dogs around the camps were barking about something. Kate shivered in the night chill and thought about what John had said.

Like him, she wasn't the same person that had left home back east. She, too, was changing. Unlike John, however, she had never felt that she had her life mapped out. She was longing to have God help her find His will for her life. Strangely enough, this sounded like something John wanted too, although he hadn't exactly said so.

"Been waitin' fer ye young people," Arkansas announced, swiping his bushy beard with a dingy blue sleeve after downing some coffee. "Thought ye might enjoy this story." The mountain man sat cross-legged in the dirt in his deerskin pants, the beaded moccasins barely visible underneath his folded legs.

"I want to tell ye how Scott's Bluff got its name. Seems a man named Hiram Scott was workin' fer a William Sublette and a company named the American Fur Tradin' Company. They was actually my rivals, but don't tell no one." The sun wrinkles around the man's eyes deepened when he smiled.

"Well, this Scott fella was in charge of a pack train that was headin' toward the Green River with supplies. He got there all right, but then he got sick—too sick to ride horseback on the return trip to St. Louis."

Arkansas took a last sip of coffee and set down the tin cup.

"So two men put 'im in a bull boat and floated 'im down the Platte to near here, where they was goin' to meet the pack train. They figured he'd be well enough to ride by then. But he wasn't."

Arkansas paused. "And, guess what happened by the time they got here!"

"The pack train had already gone?" Elisha Applegate piped up.

"Right ye are, sonny. The train hadn't waited for 'em. And they were out of supplies. So, they figured that the only chance they got is to hurry after the train, but they can't travel fast with Scott. So them two wretches ups and leaves Mr. Scott to die. The next spring some traders find his scattered bones on the other side of the river."

"You mean he'd tried to follow 'em and gotten that far?" Warren Applegate asked.

"From the looks of it, boy," Arkansas responded. "So the name has stuck to this here place. It's been called Scott's Bluff ever since."

That night, before Mama blew out the candles, Kate helped her retrieve their family quilt from the wagon. The sight of it instantly brought back warm memories of the family and farm in Missouri.

Mama had made the squares of the quilt from articles of clothing worn by members of the family: Grandma Foster's pearl lace collar, Grandpa Winfield's favorite satin vest, the white handkerchief Mama had carried when she married Papa, pieces from Kate's satin christening dress, and an old navy linen shirt Jake wore as a baby.

"Mama, how did you feel when Grandma Foster died?"

"I miss her to this day, Kate. I don't know that you ever get over the death of a loved one. Why?"

"Mr. Prentiss talked about Mr. Osborne tonight. He said his death was hard on him."

"Death is hard on everybody," Mama responded.

"Joe said something good will come from it. Could that good thing be a change in a person's heart?"

Mama handed Kate her blanket with a smile. "It sure could, Kate. It sure could."

34

FORT LARAMIE

Thursday, July 13

Slowly the North Platte meandered through the foothills of the Rocky Mountains and the land of the upper Plains Indians. This morning Arkansas was riding with Kate and her family as they walked beside their wagons around a wide bend in the river. Suddenly the mountain man pointed across the river. "Look! There in that tree—a Golden Eagle!"

"Where, Arkansas?" Jake asked, as he leaped onto Caleb's back to get a better look.

Before the mountaineer had a chance to answer, Papa's voice rang out. "Jacob Winfield! I've told you! These animals can't take any more weight. Get off that ox!"

Jake quickly jumped off Caleb, grimacing at the reprimand.

Kate knew that Papa didn't usually yell at Jake like that and realized that he was more worried about their oxen than he was letting on. She watched him nudge Hannah on the right hind quarters to spur her and Eli around some dangerous Prickly Pear cacti. Their thorns could embed themselves in an ox's hooves and cause the animal to go lame. Hannah was already breathing hard, and they had miles to go before noon.

As much as she hated to think about it, Kate knew that the emigrants would lose animals on this trip. Some had already died; more would probably die. The Winfields could probably lose one ox and still make it to Oregon, maybe even two. But Papa would do everything he could to keep from losing any.

Just then Arkansas clucked at his Appaloosa. "We're almost to Laramie, folks, so I'll be movin' on up. I'm thinkin' ye'll be glad to git a bit of civilization again."

Within the hour the emigrants finally reached bustling Fort Laramie, owned and operated by the American Fur Company. Located three quarters of a mile up the Laramie River from the mouth of the North Platte in a wide open field, the outpost was surrounded by cottonwood and ash trees. Its fifteen-foot high walls had been fashioned from adobe—dirt and chopped straw moistened with water and shaped into blocks. A large American flag with its twenty-six stars fluttered in the wind over the fort, offering the weary travelers a sign of home.

"I didn't know Indians lived here," Abby commented as the Winfields approached the post's two large gates, after making camp near the river. Papa tipped his hat as they passed another emigrant family just leaving the fort. He had tucked his ax, growing duller by the day, under one arm, while Joe carried one of their spare iron tires.

Near the fort scores of birch bark wigwams dotted the landscape. Colorful blankets hung from roughly hewn poles. Iron pots with rusting handles swung over fire holes. One woman was softening a hairless buffalo hide by tugging the skin against a thick rope. Barefoot children quietly tossed long wooden darts at netted buckskin hoops.

Why, they're doing the same things we do, thought Kate. *They're cooking and making things, and playing games. How different from us are they, really?*

Close by the fort gates, a group of older Indian men haggled with two soldiers over the purchase price of buffalo pelts still tied to a pole behind a horse.

Suddenly there was an explosion of whooping and hollering from several dozen young warriors, who were galloping back and forth in fields over by the river, waving their tomahawks and spears in the air as if they were in a battle.

"What is *that* about?" shouted Kate over the noise.

"Arkansas says they's a Sioux war party, gettin' ready to attack the Blackfeet, Missy," Joe replied over the din.

In spite of the heat, goose bumps ran up and down Kate's arms. Would these warriors scalp people and bring back dripping trophies of their fight like the Caws? Were these Indians really savages, as the people back East had said?

"What's that, Papa?" Jake's question jolted Kate back toward the fort. Her brother was pointing toward a square opening on an archway above the two entrance gates.

"That's a hole for talking to people outside the fort," Papa replied, "when they have to close the gates."

"State your business!" The gruff command came from an old fur trapper guarding one of the gates. He was so short Kate could have placed her elbows on his head. The corners of his mouth were a slimy brown from the tobacco that he was chewing.

"We've come to purchase supplies and use your blacksmith shop," Jacob responded sharply. "We're with the train of wagons that just arrived."

"Dr. Whitman's wagons?" The man scratched his mousy hair.

"That's right," Jacob answered.

"Well, why didn't you say so!" he replied in a much more neighborly tone. "Come on through, folks. You'll find the doctor in the captain's quarters if'n you're needin' him."

The smell of manure and smoke assaulted Kate's senses the moment she stepped through the gate. The dirt courtyard was probably 150 feet square, surrounded by small cabins built up against the fort's walls. Off to one side was a clay-walled corral, containing horses and mules flicking their tails against the flies. Three Sioux Indians sat against the corral and passed a long pipe from one to the other, its smoke curling up into the thick air. Trappers and American Fur Company employees were busily going in and out of the buildings. Kate recognized some people from the train, just coming out of a building that had a crude sign nailed over the door. It read, "Supply Store."

"There's the store," Jacob said to Abby. "Why don't you take Kate and Jake in there while Joe and I go fix this tire and see if they have a grinding stone?"

As Papa and Joe walked away, Kate felt uneasy. A second later she noticed a group of grimy fur traders playing a card game over a few barrels. They were staring straight at her and making comments to one another in a way that made her feel very uncomfortable. She was glad to step into the store.

When her eyes adjusted to the dimly lit inside, she saw muskrat skins hanging on hooks along one wall next to winter robes made out of buffalo hides. Men's cowhide boots with wooden pegged soles lined another wall. On a rickety table sat small sacks of black gunpowder. The crude shelves behind the counter held stone jars of rock salt, tobacco, and various other items. A sooty and sour smelling Franklin stove that apparently hadn't been used since the spring was in a corner.

"Seems like most of you folks are running low on supplies," the clerk commented irritably, scratching the gray beard that covered his face.

"Do you have any cornmeal?" Abby asked.

Kate grimaced. With his bare hand the clerk had just squished a cockroach scurrying up the dingy wall behind the counter.

"You're about the tenth person who's asked," he replied with a scowl, wiping his hand on his grimy apron. "I'm out of that, but I can sell you a five-pound bag of flour for $1.25."

"One dollar and twenty-five cents?" Abby shot back. "That's highway robbery! I can get a whole barrel for $4 at home."

"Well now, Ma'am, you ain't home, are you?" the man scowled. "Take it or leave it."

Abby loosened the drawstring of her velvet purse and deposited the $1.25 on the counter with a loud sigh. Kate knew what her mother was thinking. Five pounds of flour wouldn't last long, but at these prices they wouldn't be able to buy much more. Kate lifted the bag of flour and they left.

As the door slammed behind them, the card players spotted Kate and began to leer at her again. She didn't dare lift her long skirt to keep it out of the mud now. "Mama, let's get out of here," she whispered. Abby nodded her head, and they quickened their pace.

Just outside the gate, they met up with Jacob and Ole Joe and Dr. Whitman, who had finished meeting with the fort's commander.

"That was nothing but a fur trading post," Jacob lamented on their way back. "They weren't prepared for the likes of us. They didn't even have a grinding stone."

"Jacob, I'm getting worried," Abby spoke up. "All they had was this five-pound bag of flour, and they charged us an outrageous price for it. We're completely out of meat now and dried fruit. We're low on flour and sugar. And the cornmeal is going bad. What are we going to do?" Worry lines were etched across her mother's face.

Kate waited for Papa's response. If they ran out of food in the wilderness, what *would* they do? Oregon was still a couple of months away. Where would they find food without a store?

"The doctor here says there's another fort ahead, Abby," Jacob replied, tightening his lips. "It's called Bridger. Maybe they'll have more."

"What if that fort is just a trading fort, too?"

"I'm afraid she has a point, Jacob," Dr. Whitman spoke up. "After William Sublette built this place, the American Fur Company bought it to trade furs and other things with the Indians, not to supply emigrants. They weren't prepared for the likes of us. But, if my hunch is right, they had better get ready to do that. In fact, he and I were just discussing it."

A question had been lurking in the back of Kate's mind for some time, and as they approached their camp near the river, she decided to ask it. "Doctor," she began, "do you think a lot of people like us will be coming?"

Whitman pulled a dingy handkerchief out of his shirt pocket and tugged off his black brimmed hat. "Kate, we're just seeing the beginning of what's going to happen to this land. There'll be more people. Plenty more." He mopped his brow.

Kate went on. "What do you think will happen to these Indians when others come?"

The doctor paused for a moment. "I really don't know, Kate. They may gradually lose their way of life."

For the rest of the day, Kate couldn't get Dr. Whitman's comment off her mind. She wondered: Could losing their way of life be a good thing?

35

BALAK

Wednesday, July 19

Kate wondered if she would ever get free of the dust. Like everyone else, she had tied a bandanna over her nose and mouth so she could breathe, but the dust had covered her clothes, her bonnet, her hands, the back of her neck, and now had even gotten into her boots.

The dust was so thick that the visibility was only about ten feet. From where she was walking, beside the big wagon's left front wheel, she could not even see the lead pair of oxen, Hannah and Eli. Nor could she see Joe, coming along behind with the supply wagon. She hoped he was still there. The rest of the family looked like ghosts, covered as they were with white powder.

Ever since the emigrants had left Fort Laramie, the trail to Oregon had been slowly rising through the foothills of the Rocky Mountains. It was an unforgiving land—dry and parched with sparse vegetation. And now, churned up by thousands of hooves and hundreds of wagon wheels, the trail had turned to dust.

In the stifling heat the dust hung over the wagon train like a moving cloud. Driven by the constant wind, it forced its way into their clothes, their hair, their food, their bedding—everything they owned. The emigrants tied bandannas or kerchiefs over their noses and mouths so they could breathe, but there was no way to keep it out of their eyes, or the eyes of their animals.

To make things worse, for the last several days the dust had turned deadly. The ground was covered with unavoidable patches of white salt, which got mixed into the dust and burned when it coated open spots of skin. Alkali—poisonous to both people and animals.

The oxen began to give out more frequently now, going blind from the alkali dust and having to be shot, or just dying from sheer exhaustion. This caused delays and slowdowns and scattered the wagons more than ever.

Tempers were flaring. Some emigrants wanted to go faster while others insisted on taking it slow because of their animals. Arguments could be heard between husbands and wives over having to discard belongings to lighten the load on the oxen. Each day Kate spotted dead animals and things cast aside: a headboard, a trunk, an iron stove. The trail was becoming littered with the sad reminders of people's losses.

Kate kept repeating to herself a verse from the Bible that Dr. Whitman had read last Sunday morning. As the rose-streaked light of morning came up over the hills to the east, he had begun a brief worship service with words of comfort from Psalm 46: "God is our refuge and our strength, a very present help in time of trouble."

I sure hope you are "a present help" with us, God, Kate thought, *because our troubles are definitely growing.*

"Kate, my eyes hurt," complained Jake.

"I know, Jake, mine do too," responded Kate. "There's nothing we can do about it until the nooning. Then we can wash the dust out. But don't rub them—you'll make it worse!"

Arkansas and John Gantt, the pilot, had warned everyone that the alkali was poisonous, and that it was in the water in these parts, even in the rivers. Dr. Whitman had told people to test the water before they drank it or let their animals drink it.

On the day it happened, the Winfields had stopped for the nooning. Papa had released Balak from his U-shaped bar first. While Papa and Joe unhitched the others, the thirsty Balak spied a small but tempting pond nestled near some green willows. He ambled over while Papa wasn't looking.

Kate looked up from knocking dust off some food sacks and saw Balak's unassuming brown form near that pond. She heard the lapping noise of his tongue, happily drinking the water, and suddenly realized what was happening.

"Papa," she yelled. "Stop him!"

The other oxen's chains clanked as Jacob and Joe dropped them and dashed toward the pond. Joe slapped the ox on the hindquarters, first with his hat and then with his hands, while Papa screamed "Balak, get out of there!" and yanked on the ox's horns.

With an attitude that asked why he was being yelled at, Balak raised his big black eyes, shrugged his broad shoulders, flicked the flies off his hind end, and moved away from the pond.

But it was too late.

Three hours later, their temperamental and hard-working ox died.

As the family stood over Balak's body saying goodbye, Jake asked "What'll we do now, Papa?"

"We don't have any choice," Papa said grimly. "We'll have to give up the supply wagon and leave it here—we don't have enough oxen to haul it anymore. I'll have to use six oxen on the big wagon, same as before. The extra one can follow behind the wagon with Midnight and Tess, and we'll rotate it into the team each day. We'll yoke Prudence with Balaam to start."

Later that afternoon, when they were finally able to get moving again, Kate trudged along in the dust, plagued by questions that kept swirling around in her head. Wasn't there something they could have done? Wasn't there some treatment they could have given the poor ox? The questions kept nagging at her, questions for which she had no answers.

She soon discovered that they weren't the only family that had lost livestock from alkali poisoning that day, because they passed many other dead oxen and cattle that afternoon.

The sight that stayed in Kate's mind for a long time after that day, however, was that of their supply wagon, stripped of its wheels, turned on its side, and abandoned. The lonely little wagon seemed to plead with Kate not to leave it there all by itself, but in a few more steps it was obscured in clouds of swirling dust.

Not long after that, John Prentiss rode by to offer his condolences on the loss of Balak. But he also had some tragic news to share that had saddened everyone who had learned of it.

"Did you Winfields hear about Joel Hembree?" John asked as he slowly rode along beside the big wagon.

"No. What is it?" responded Kate.

"He died this afternoon, just after two o'clock."

Kate's hand flew to her mouth as her heart sank. Joel had been a bright and happy boy, a delight to everyone who knew him.

Abby cried out, "Oh my! How did it happen?"

"Just after they left Laramie," John said, switching the reins to his other hand, "he hopped up on the tongue of their wagon while it was moving. A jolt knocked him off, and he fell under the front wheel and then the back one ran over him. They sent for Dr. Whitman, but the boy was crushed so badly that there was nothing the doc could do but keep him comfortable until he died."

Tears began to well up in Kate's eyes. "I'm sure his parents are devastated."

"I thought you'd want to know. They're going to bury him tomorrow. I'd better get back to our wagon, but I'll see you there."

As John rode off, a deep sadness came over Kate. This was the second death on the wagon train.

The elephant was getting much larger.

God, why did you let that little boy die? Kate thought as she walked on. *What is the purpose in that? And why did Balak have to die? He wasn't hurting anybody—he was just doing what he normally does, being an ox and drinking water.*

Kate quickly realized she didn't understand any of this, and that whatever faith in God she had was surely on shaky ground now.

Yet, into her mind came Joe's words: "Ye've got to hold onto yer thoughts, Missy."

Kate tried to lasso her thoughts and bring them back into faith.

It didn't seem to be working.

36

RATTLER!

Thursday, July 27

Papa and Joe had yoked the oxen, and the Winfields were just about ready to start the day's journey.

"We've come a long way, Jake," Kate said, tying her bonnet tightly under her chin. "We got across the North Platte last Saturday without any trouble, and now we're already in the front range of the Rocky Mountains, thousands of feet higher than it was at home. Papa says we're headed over to the Sweetwater River now. It's a tributary of the North Platte." Kate's words were an attempt to encourage herself as well her brother.

"Arkansas says we should get to Independence Rock sometime this afternoon," Jacob added, as he fetched his riding crop out of the wagon.

"I ain't seen no roads yet," Jake complained.

"That's *any* roads yet, Jake. And you won't," countered Abby, securing the rocker to the back of the wagon with rope. "There aren't any."

"I bet you this'll be a road one day," Jake said smugly.

"What makes you say that, Jake?" Jacob asked, swiping at the gnats.

"'Cause we saw those guv'ment men again yesterday when we got here. They was taking notes and looking at some metal tube on three legs." Jake and his pals, the Applegate twins, had been spying things out.

"That tube is a barometer, Jake. They were using it to try and figure out how high we are above sea level," Papa told him. "And I think you mean Mr. Fremont."

"Yep, he's the one. He's making a map for the guv'ment. Warren told me so."

"For heaven's sake, Jake, it's *government*, not guv'ment," his mother scolded. "You can talk better than that!"

"The boy might be right about the road, Abby," Jacob mused out loud. "Now, wouldn't *that* be something. We'd be the first ones to blaze the trail!"

"Ready, Joe?" he yelled to his old hired hand, who was standing on the other side of the ox team. "Let's move!" Papa said to Prudence and Balaam, laying the riding crop on their hindquarters. The two faithful oxen, whose turn it was once again to be in the lead, leaned into their yoke, and the Winfield wagon moved out of their campsite to join the rest of the emigrants.

"All the oxen are working together in different pairs pretty well, Mama," Kate remarked to her mother. But, as she retied her bandanna over her nose and mouth, she wondered if Balaam missed Balak as much as she did.

That afternoon the wagons of the Oregon Emigrating Company rumbled toward the Sweetwater River across a bleak and desolate landscape of red sandstone buttes, seemingly inhabited by nothing except antelope. As far as Kate could see, when she could see at all through the choking alkali dust, there was no vegetation. She couldn't imagine what the bounding animals lived on.

When they reached the river, they followed it to the northwest for a few more hours, and then stopped for the night on a high plateau that was separated from the surrounding land by steep clay-colored slopes.

"You mean the water isn't sweet?" Jake was clearly disappointed, as Joe came back from the river with two sloshing buckets of water.

"Well, Mistah Jake," Joe smiled as he set them down. "That all depends on what ye mean by 'sweet'. Seems to me that river's mountain water is pretty sweet, 'specially after the last couple of weeks."

"Guess you're right there, Joe," Jake laughed as he sipped some water from a ladle.

"Arkansas told me how the river got its name, Joe," Kate offered, taking the ladle from her brother. "Said a fur trapper's mule fell in the stream and lost a big pack of sugar." The liquid trickled down her parched throat. "But he thought the river would've gotten the name anyways, because anyone crossing the alkali basin would think this was sweet."

"Kate." Jake changed the subject abruptly. "Want to go climb the rock after supper? You can ask Jane, and I'll get Warren and Elisha."

Kate silently wished she could go with John but decided that she needed to do something with her brother. Her mother's nod confirmed her decision.

"Sure, Jake," Kate responded and added, "We'll take Scout."

After supper, with Scout leading the way, the young people hiked across the barren ground toward a large granite dome that looked to be several thousand feet long and almost a thousand feet wide.

"It looks like a giant turtle," said Warren, which met with general agreement from everyone. When they got closer they could see that the "turtle" had plenty of crevices and cracks in its "shell" that offered the young people plenty of places to grip as they climbed up.

Scout reached the top first and sat, waiting for the others with his tongue hanging out. Within minutes the group had joined him. The view from the top was well worth the climb—they could see the entire wagon train spread out below. From afar the rock indeed resembled a great turtle, but from above it looked just like boulders stacked neatly on top of one another by a giant unseen hand.

"They call it Independence Rock because a fur trapper arrived here on Independence Day back in '24," Elisha offered.

"Look at all the names carved here," Jake exclaimed. "Bill Sublette; M.K. Hugh, 1824," he read. "Nat Wyeth, 1842—that's just last year!"

"Let's add our names," Warren suggested. "I brought my Papa's knife." He tugged the Bowie knife out of its leather sheath and began chipping at the rock.

"Do it quickly, boys," urged Kate. "The sun's going down fast now, and we'd best be getting back."

Jane and Kate talked while they waited for the boys.

"How are things with William?" Kate asked, as she shook out her calico skirt.

"Father and Mother like him, Kate. I think I love him. He's everything I could want in a husband. Kind. Industrious. Full of hope."

"That's wonderful, Jane. I'm really happy for you." Kate plucked off her bonnet to let the breeze blow through her auburn hair.

"How about you and John?" Jane asked with a slight nudge. "I saw you two talking together at Scott's Bluff."

Kate laughed. "We had a nice talk, but that was all there was to it. He doesn't know what he wants to do with his life."

As Kate and Jane wound their way through a gully on the way back to camp, the boys lingered behind to catch fireflies. Scout was just in front of the girls as they approached a large rock. Suddenly he stopped and sniffed the air. With one sharp bark, he jumped around the rock and disappeared.

"Scout, come back here!" Kate yelled and hurried after him.

As Kate was rounding the rock, she heard a rattling buzz and a loud yelp. She saw Scout lying in the dirt, whining in pain as he furiously licked at his front right foreleg. Just a few feet away, a large gray snake with diamonds on its back was slithering away, satisfied at having taken care of its enemy. Scout had been bitten by a rattler!

Scooping Scout up into her arms, Kate quickly ran for the camp, calling at the top of her lungs for Dr. Whitman. Jane and the boys followed as fast as they could.

A few moments later Kate held her whimpering dog down, while Dr. Whitman quickly found the puncture wounds. Cutting open Scout's leg, he said to Kate: "He's fortunate you got him here as fast as you did; much later and he might not have made it." Sucking on the wound, he spat out the venom and blood, and then retrieved a small sack of plantain leaves from his bag. "The Indians chew these into a poultice," he explained, putting several in his mouth.

As the doctor tied the moistened leaves onto the wound with a strip of cloth, Jane said quietly, "You know, Kate, Scout may have saved your life. If he hadn't warned you, you would have walked around that rock and right into that rattler!"

"I agree," added Dr. Whitman. "The Almighty is looking out for you, young lady. You can be sure of that!"

As she curled up around a sleeping Scout that night, Kate marveled at what had happened. She had saved this dog's life, and now Scout had saved hers. It certainly did look like God was watching out for her. What did it all mean?

37

SOUTH PASS

Friday–Thursday, July 28–August 10

The scenery became spectacular as the Company followed the Sweetwater upstream and higher into the hills. Shortly after leaving Independence Rock, they came to a narrow canyon called Devil's Gate, where the rushing river flowed between three hundred-foot walls of towering granite. Off in the distance another granite formation called Split Rock had a V-shaped opening at its peak that looked as if some giant had taken an ax to it. As the Company traveled, to the right they could see snow-covered mountains in the distance.

They had entered a land of extreme contrasts. Away from the river, the land was dry and parched with patches of alkali salts and no vegetation except sagebrush. The days were brutally hot—sometimes over 100 degrees—with no shade at all.

The nights, on the other hand, had turned quite cold. Often the temperature dropped below freezing, and Kate would have to break through ice in the water barrel to make coffee in the morning. Fortunately there was enough grass along the river for the animals, and the hunters were able to find some game—antelope and elk out on the sagebrush flats and sage hens that came to the river to drink. Joe said that was "God's provision."

Scout's leg didn't swell a great deal, indicating that the snake hadn't injected much venom. After limping for about a week, the dog quickly regained his spunky self and happily ambled along beside Kate once again. She knew he was completely well when he resumed chasing the white-tailed prairie dogs out on the flats, which poked their heads out of their burrows watching for eagles and falcons.

On August 7 the Oregon Emigrating Company neared South Pass, "the backbone of this here land," as Arkansas put it. Kate had pointed out to Jake that after South Pass the rivers would all flow west; they would be at the top of the continent.

But the approach to South Pass was a long gentle rise, so gentle that it was hard to tell that the ground was rising at all. Jake couldn't believe it. He kept running ahead of the wagons, and calling back, "Kate, am I higher than you now?"

They wouldn't have known they had crossed the pass at all if John Gantt had not ridden to each group of wagons, telling everyone that they were now more than eight hundred and thirty miles from Missouri and were officially entering the Oregon Territory. But they were not yet halfway to the Pacific Ocean.

Another great loss befell the train on the ninth of August. The Winfields' friend Ed Stevenson passed away with a high fever. While wiping his neck, Kate had found a black tick, leading Dr. Whitman to wonder if perhaps the insect had carried a disease. The Winfields and the other families had helped a devastated Catherine bury her husband on the bank of a creek. Hidden under large stones laid over his grave to guard it from the wolves, a small chiseled rock read:

EDWARD JAMES STEVENSON
1811–1843

While her parents didn't say much about Mr. Stevenson's death, Kate could tell they were upset about it. Papa's turquoise eyes gazed into the distance more often, and Mama regularly visited Catherine, either while they were walking or during their stops. Her friend had been left without a husband to help her, so Papa and Mama determined to do everything they could to see that Catherine arrived in Oregon safely.

Across ravines and around hollows the journey continued. It seemed endless now, through a hot and dry country, except for the welcome relief of the Green River. While the company made ready to ford the river, Kate watched two Great Blue herons forage for insects along the river bank.

The emigrants forded the Green River without incident, although Jake remarked that it sure didn't look green to him.

Then the trail became dry and sandy again for several days. Many families were having trouble with shrinking wagon wheels, which caused the iron tires to slip off.

At one nooning, as soon as the wagons stopped rolling, Kate saw her father, coughing from the morning's trail dust, bend down to look at the big wagon's right front wheel.

"Abby, I'm afraid we're going to be here a few hours, 'til Joe and I can fix this blamed wheel again." He erupted in a long fit of coughing.

"Papa, are you all right?" Kate asked.

"Yep, I'm all right, but this wheel sure ain't," he replied unhappily. "That tire won't stay on there two more miles! Maybe you and your mother can rustle up something to eat while Joe and I get to work on the wheel," he added. "Jake, you help Joe with building us a fire, and I'll cut some shims."

Jacob quickly cut down a small ash sapling several inches thick and began to carve flexible strips from it with his Bowie knife. After they downed a quick meal of cornmeal biscuits and dried buffalo jerky, Joe put the iron tire in the fire and heated it while Jacob tied the ash strips to the wheel with strips of buffalo hide that had been soaked in water. When the tire was red hot, Jacob asked "Have you got the water ready, Kate?"

"All ready, Papa," she responded, holding a wooden bucket filled to the brim.

"Joe, bring the tire over to the wheel, and we'll knock it on. And as soon as we tell you, Kate, throw the water on that tire—two times. 'Cause if we don't get that tire cooled in a hurry, it'll burn through the shims and we'll have fixed nothin'."

Joe picked up the tire with a pair of sticks and carried it quickly over to the wheel, where Jacob knocked it on over the ash shims with the butt end of his ax.

"Now, Kate!" Jacob called, jumping away from the wheel.

Steam hissed up violently when Kate sloshed the water on the hot iron the first time. But the second time there was much less steam.

"I think it's working," Jacob announced, relief in his voice. But this has got to hold until we get to Oregon. We can't keep driving wedges between the tire and this wheel. They're not going to hold it together."

38

HORSE THIEVES

Monday, August 14

The wagons had headed southwest toward Fort Bridger, which had felt like the wrong way, since Oregon was to the northwest. However John Gantt had assured them that the detour would be worth it, since Fort Bridger had a blacksmith shop. As Kate's mother had told her father, "I'm still hoping Gantt knows what he's doing, Jacob."

Located on a grassy plain close by the Green River, Fort Bridger was not an impressive sight. A stockade fence of logs covered with sun-baked mud protected several crudely constructed log cabins, including one that served as the general store, post office, and barracks.

"Looks pretty shabby to me, Jacob," Abby remarked, as Papa brought the oxen to a halt next to the other wagons in their small company.

"At least there's plenty of grass for the animals," Kate offered.

"That's true, Kate, and firewood and water, too," Papa said with a smile.

But other than a little lard and coffee, a small supply of gunpowder, and iron to make replacements for wheel rims, the emigrants found few supplies to purchase.

A few hours later, when Ole Joe returned from the blacksmith shop rolling a wagon wheel with a new iron rim, he reported that the traders at the fort were talking about a recent raid by Sioux and Cheyenne Indians, who had run off all the buffalo, killed three Snake Indians, and stolen sixty horses!

Abby and Kate looked up anxiously from their supper preparations. "Don't worry, ladies," Papa said. "They won't attack us—it's the horses and cattle they want. But we'd better post extra guards tonight on our animals."

"Joe, if you'll put this repaired wheel back on its axle, I'll go make sure Peter Burnett knows about this."

That night Kate went to bed early and slept soundly, until Scout awakened her. He was whining just outside the tent.

"What's the matter, boy?" she whispered. He whined some more and then growled. Kate decided to go out and have a look.

The pale light of a nearly full moon showed nothing wrong, and the only sound was the chorus of crickets. But Scout was obviously disturbed about something. With his nose to the ground, he began sniffing his way out toward the meadow where the horses were tethered. Kate followed.

"Must be some elk in with the horses." The male voice startled Kate. She had forgotten that Mr. Applegate had posted guards around the horses now. She stopped beside a pine tree and listened.

"Seeing antlers are we, Atkins?" This voice sounded familiar—it was Lancefield Johnson. "Those horses aren't going anywhere. The tethers will hold them."

"They might be elk," Atkins went on. "Hard to tell. Horses don't seem bothered though. Say, what is all that growling?"

"It's a dog," Johnson quickly realized. "Hey, dog, get outta here. You'll scare the—"

Just at that moment Scout began barking furiously.

And instantly the dark exploded into a pandemonium of noises. Wild whoops and cries erupted from the horse pasture, followed instantly by the squealing and screaming of horses. Kate heard the sound of hooves pounding the dirt, and then a group of frightened horses flew by her, with three dark figures riding bareback close behind. Each of the figures was wearing an animal skin with antlers on his head, yelling an Indian battle cry. With his ears laid back, Scout raced after them, barking at the top of his lungs.

"Indians!" Johnson yelled as he fired at the fleeing riders. As his shot echoed in Kate's ears, Atkins also fired, but both men missed. "Indians!" cried Atkins. "They're stealing our horses!"

By now the entire camp was thoroughly roused. After the horses were accounted for, the men discovered that the Cheyenne had only managed to steal eight horses—three chestnuts, two geldings, a sorrel, and a stallion. As they discussed the night's events, Jesse Applegate appeared, dragging behind him an elk skin with the antlers still attached.

"One of them must have dropped this," he announced.

"That's how they do it," John Gantt responded. "They wear an elk skin, with the antlers on their heads, and crawl in among the horses. If the guards look in their direction, they think it's just elk in grazing with the horses. Then they cut the horses' tethers, jump on the backs of a few, yell like crazy, and drive all the rest before them. They've been known to steal thirty and forty at a time!"

Scout was hailed as a hero. As Mr. Johnson told the men the next day, "If Miss Winfield's dog hadn't raised the alarm, the Cheyenne would have gotten three times as many horses!"

39

ABBY

Saturday, August 19

The Oregon Emigrating Company pulled out of Fort Bridger and headed northwest again, into the valley of the Bear River. The early morning sun flecked off the river's surface as it coursed in a northerly direction toward a place called Soda Springs.

"Reminds me of the Platte," Abby commented quietly as she untied her dingy sky blue bonnet with one hand and swiped the perspiration off her brow with the other. "Wide. Shallow. Easy." Her words seemed slow to Kate today, like the river.

"A man could almost put down roots here," Jacob commented. "The soil's rich."

Kate stepped around a cluster of Blue Flag irises. The morning air was cool today, she thought, as she watched river otters jumping into the water from a bank nearby.

"Papa, can we catch some fish tonight?" Jake scurried forward. "Warren says him and his brother caught six mountain trout last night and fried 'em in a pan. Said they were the best eatin' ever."

"Trout sounds good to me," Papa replied. "What d'ya say, Abby?" The gait in Mama's walk had slowed down.

"She can't hear you, Papa," Kate offered. "She's behind us. Probably looking for some flowers for tonight."

As the wagons rolled on, Kate turned back to find her mother.

"Mama, how come you're way back here?" Kate asked.

Her mother didn't look good. Her eyes were hollow and sunken into her face and her skin looked chalky blue. "Mama, are you all right?"

Abby's long calico skirt, tattered and stained from months on the trail, bunched up as she hunched over and clutched her stomach. "My stomach's aching something fierce, Kate. I must've eaten something bad."

"What should we do?"

"Ask Papa to wait for me. I might need to ride today."

The wagon creaked as Kate scrambled inside to arrange a place for her mother. There wasn't much room for a person to lie down in the ten-foot-by-four-foot wagon bed. Kate clambered over the clothing, food sacks, the trunk, and the two straight-back chairs to grab her quilt. Stretched over everything, it would make a lumpy kind of pallet, but at least it was a place where Mama could lie down.

Where was their medical satchel? Kate rummaged around the wagon and finally found it.

After helping her mother inside the wagon, Kate drew the puckering strings together for privacy. "I just need to rest, Kate." Abby's words sounded more like a groan.

"I'll check back on you in a little while then, Mama," Kate said.

In the meantime she had to figure out what was wrong. She flipped through the pages of the medical book: Headache. Muscle cramps. Sunken eyes. Bad color. Kate found entries about the use of Alfalfa and Aloe Vera and even Black Cohosh. She and Mama had tinctures for the first two, so that was good. Catnip was also used for digestion and Golden Seal could be used both internally and externally. Kate was feeling a bit better; at least they had some choices.

A few minutes later Jake poked his head into the swaying bonnet and then back out. "Kate, Mama's asking for water. Can I get her a cup?" Kate handed Jake the tin cup.

Then it happened. A moan so unlike Mama that it made the hairs on the back of Kate's neck stand up.

"Kate, check on your Mama," Jacob hollered from his position next to the lead oxen.

Papa didn't have to tell her. Something wasn't right. Mama was never sick, and if she felt bad, she rarely said so. Kate's mother believed that a woman had to be strong; complaining about an ache or ailment only made matters worse. For Mama to cry out like this meant she was very sick.

This alarmed Kate all the more. She hastily climbed onto the backboard.

"Jake, fetch me the bucket quick! Mama's starting to vomit."

Kate knew that Mama's body was trying to get rid of something. But what? And why?

She tried to stay focused. Vomiting. Thirst. Now her skin was cold. What would cause all of this?

And so fast.

Too fast.

Kate decided on a tincture that included ginger. With every sip her mother would not take, Kate's fears grew.

"Please, Mama, just a small sip," Kate pleaded.

Abby's head turned away. Kate knew she had to get some kind of liquid into her mother. She couldn't let Mama get dehydrated, because that might kill her. Yet, try as she might, Kate couldn't get her mother to drink more than a drop of the liquid.

An hour later Kate made the decision. "Papa," Kate's voice carried easily to her Papa, who was pacing behind the backboard now. "Where's Doc Whitman?"

"He's trying to settle an argument between two of the cattle guards last night. Should I send Jake to fetch him?"

"Yep. Something's not right. Mama's too sick."

"I've been thinking the same thing." Papa hardly got the last word out before he was hollering for Jake.

Dr. Whitman arrived just after they stopped the wagons for the noonday meal.

"Sorry it took so long, Jacob," he explained as he dismounted and handed Jake the reins. "I came as soon as the boy found me. Joe, would you fetch my medical kit? It's tied on my horse."

"Doc, she's awful sick now. She's even talking crazy." Jacob's words came fast. Kate could hear the worry in his voice. "We don't know what to do. Kate's inside with her."

A short while later, the doctor crawled out of the wagon. What happened next seemed to happen in slow motion. Dr. Whitman unbuttoned the top button of his bib front shirt, as if he were really hot, and slowly ran his fingers through his thin black hair. Then he placed his hand on Papa's shoulder and uttered the most horrible word he could have said: cholera.

That was the word that struck terror in every heart that ever heard it.

Cholera.

The disease that killed thousands, often in twenty-four hours, sometimes even quicker. The disease that now held her mother in its deathly grip.

"I'm not sure," the doctor had said. "But that's what it looks like."

Kate's boots were glued to the dirt. She couldn't move. For a long moment she couldn't even breathe. Surely this wasn't happening. Things like this only occurred in bad dreams. This had to be a bad dream.

She dimly heard the doctor tell Papa there wasn't anything he could do. "Her fever's very high, Jacob. I'll try to keep her comfortable."

Terror gripped Kate's heart. "There has to be something we can do, Doc!" she blurted out. "There just has to be. I'll get her to drink something. I'll force it down her if I have to. She can pull through this. She's strong. She's never sick!" Kate was almost wailing the words now.

"I'm sorry, Kate. I wish I knew something that could cure it, but I don't. You've done everything I would've done. We don't know a lot about this, Kate, except that it's very contagious. So, you can't go back in there now. I'll watch her."

The next few hours blurred into one long afternoon of wagons passing them by. Joe managed the team, trying to keep the wagon from jostling too much while they drove slowly on.

The word traveled fast through the wagon train. As the wagons passed, the men tipped their hats to Papa, and the women held their hands together as a sign that they were praying. The long faces of the children told Kate that now even they knew.

Around 3 p.m. the doctor directed Jacob to halt the wagon after examining Abby. "She's breathing heavy, Jacob," he said, with great sorrow in his voice. "Best to say your goodbyes now."

The doctor's silver watch read 4:32 when Abigail Foster Winfield breathed her last breath.

40

GRIEVING

Saturday Evening, August 19

As the golden hues deepened in the western sky, the Winfields held vigil at their camp around the fire. Slowly their fellow emigrants began to appear, carrying lighted tallow candles that cast soft shadows on the bonnet of the Winfield wagon. Some of their visitors brought wild flowers, and some brought dishes of whatever food they had to share. Betsy Applegate arrived with trail bread and Jane Mills brought beans and rice. Others just came—Reverend Garrison, Mr. and Mrs. Lenox, Mr. Hembree, Captain Gantt. And late that night, even the Burnetts from the Light Column, which was miles away.

Catherine Stevenson stayed to help prepare Mama for burial. Mrs. Stevenson told Kate she didn't care whether it was contagious or not, because Kate's mother had been her friend, and she was going to help her friend. Mrs. Stevenson told Kate what to do and Kate simply obeyed. The two women dressed Abby in her special plaid dress, the one with the scooped bodice and puffed sleeves. Kate combed her Mama's wavy black locks and tied a front bow in the silk ribbon around her head.

It was a beautiful star-lit night, but Kate didn't notice. When John Prentiss and Jesse Applegate offered to dig the grave, she was able to say "thank you," but nothing more.

She felt numb.

As Joe played a sorrowful tune on his fiddle, Kate managed to respond to those who offered their condolences with "we appreciate it" and "thank you for coming," but that was all.

Most of the time she sat, rocking back and forth. All she really wanted to do was sleep—sleep and never wake up again. Kate felt that her heart had broken in pieces and that most of it had died with her mother, and she would never get it back.

Rocking—back and forth, back and forth.

Then she remembered. Mama's rocking chair. Where was it?

Kate looked over at the big wagon, and there it was—sitting next to the back wagon wheel, exactly where Papa had placed it.

Alone, and still . . . holding a vigil of its own . . . waiting.

For Mama.

Kate couldn't bring herself to sit in her Mama's rocker. As the night progressed and the visitors left, Kate finally found herself sitting next to Ole Joe. Jake crawled over and put his head in her lap. Her brother's thick hair felt grimy from the trail dust as she stroked it, but Kate didn't care. The hurt they were both feeling was far greater than dirt or grime. This was a hurt that nothing could wash away.

Papa grieved alone beside his wife's carefully wrapped body, which lay next to the wagon, awaiting burial. He sat against a wagon wheel with his head down against his knees.

Joe carefully put down his horsehair bow in the soft velvet top of his battered case. "Yer Mama was a mighty fine woman, Miz Kate," their wise old hand began in his deep voice, a voice that was both familiar and soothing to Kate. "She always took good care of me and treated me with respect. I know ye're gonna miss her somethin' terrible."

He went on. "But ye'll always have her right here. In yer heart." His fingers pointed at his chest. "I will, too."

The clasp on the fiddle's case clicked in the night air when he closed it. Joe paused; the seconds became minutes. The breeze rustling the leaves and the night sounds of the cattle would normally have created a sense of peace for Kate.

But not on this night. None of this could be real—it just couldn't. Couldn't someone please do something to make it all go away?

"I wish I knew what to say to make ye feel better, Missy. Nobody can say nothin'." Joe's voice sounded far away. "When I lost my Bessie, nothin' made me feel better. Only God can help us with this kind of pain. But it takes time."

The next morning Jacob Winfield and his family buried their beloved Abigail in a place where the summer cottonwoods shaded the lush Bear River Valley.

It was a Sunday. The Lord's Day.

And now, it would forever be Mama's day, too.

41

FORT HALL

Monday, August 28

Kate drank in the scene with her eyes: the Company's animals were grazing contentedly amidst the lush grasses waving gently in the morning wind and drinking from the numerous small springs and creeks that dotted the wide valley. Though the day would turn much warmer, there was a chill in the air that promised the soon arrival of fall.

"Sure am sorry to hear about Miz Abby, Mr. Winfield." The raspy voice could belong to no one other than Arkansas. Kate hadn't seen the mountain man since before her mother died. "Jest heard when I got back," he said, reining his spotted Appaloosa into a stop next to their wagon. He whisked off a beaver cap to reveal his shoulder-length hair, unkempt as always. "Was scoutin' the trail ahead."

"I appreciate you stopping by, Saw," responded her father. His voice had a flat and lifeless tone to it.

It had been that way every day since Mama died, thought Kate. He still drove the wagon and took care of the oxen and stayed involved in the Company. But he wasn't the same.

In the evening, when she was fixing supper, Kate would see him leaning against a tree with his hands in his pockets, gazing quietly at the river and the sunset. Or late at night, if she had to get up, she would find him staring into the fire, unable to sleep. Joe had told her that her father was grieving too, the same as she was, but in his own way. It seemed that part of Papa had died too.

"How does it look ahead?" Jacob asked.

"Trail gonna be hard along the Snake." The old trapper offered Jacob and Joe his gnarled hand to shake. "Not much game. Tough, dusty country."

More sand and sagebrush and long dusty days? Kate didn't want to hear about it.

"This here Snake River," Jake pointed toward the nearby winding river, "got its name 'cuz it snakes around a lot. Ain't that right, Arkansas?"

"Jake, we already told you that's why it's called that!" Kate sounded irritated. For the last couple of weeks, she hadn't had very much patience. Even the little things bothered her, like her brother's ten-year-old questions.

When they had camped at Soda Springs, he had almost driven her crazy. The springs were a place where warm mineral-laden water burst out of holes in the ground every few seconds. The water tasted like soda, but Jake had to know why.

"Why does it taste like soda?" he had asked.

"What makes the rock spit out the water?"

"Why do the trappers call this one Beer Springs?"

On and on, every answer leading to another question. The questions persisted throughout the five-day journey to Fort Hall, where the emigrants were now gratefully encamped in a beautiful valley.

"You folks been up to the fort yet?" Arkansas went on.

"Not yet," Papa replied. "We need some supplies, though."

"I'd be a might pleased to escort Miz Kate, if'n ye'd like. I'll take her to the store."

As Kate and Arkansas rode the mile from the camp up to Fort Hall, their horses picked their way through the fields among hundreds of buffalo skulls bleaching in the sun, an ancient graveyard of weathered horns and hollow eye sockets.

"Arkansas, why are all these skulls here?"

"Buffalo used to live here, Ma'am, long time ago. Died here, too."

The adobe-covered log walls of Fort Hall were situated 150 yards from the south bank of the Snake River. From a corner bastion of the fort, Kate could see a British flag fluttering in the breeze. She didn't feel much like making conversation, but she was curious about the flag.

"Is this fort British, Arkansas?"

"Yep. Nat Wyeth built her to supply the fur trappers, but then in '38 he sold her to the Hudson Bay Comp'ny. Cap'n Grant runs things here."

"What are those?" Kate pointed to some rotting wagons scattered to one side of the field.

"Them's wagons people left behind," the trapper replied, guiding his horse Red a few feet further away from Midnight.

Broken wagon wheels caused the decaying wagons to tilt in crazy directions. Weeds were growing up through the wagon beds, and torn bonnets flapped in the ever-present wind. Kate thought of how their owners had dreamt of taking these wagons all the way to the Pacific Ocean. Their wagons had ended up here, now slowly being destroyed by the sun and rain and weeds. It was a field of broken dreams, just like her mother's death had broken their family's dream of a new life together in Oregon. Kate turned her head away.

"Only a few loaded wagons has ever made it this fer, Miz Kate," Arkansas continued as their horses whinnied a greeting to the horses at the fort. "Ye're among the first. Cap'n Grant tells folks to leave their wagons here. He cain't see how a wagon can make it through the mountains up ahead. I'm 'spectin' he'll tell you folks the same thing. If ye take yer wagons on, ye'll be the very first to ever do it." Arkansas scratched at his scruffy chin as if the thought was worth remembering.

Kate didn't much care about being first to do anything. She wasn't even sure she cared about making the rest of this trip without Mama. But they couldn't stay here, and she couldn't think only of herself. Papa and Jake needed her help to go on.

The horses drew up to a hitching rail outside the fort. As Kate slid down out of the saddle and tied Midnight to the rail, she turned and looked at the grizzled old mountain man.

"Arkansas, do you think we can make it?" she asked quietly.

His eyes softened, and he paused for a moment. Then his answer was cautious. "I 'spect so, miss. I 'spect so."

Inside the fort's gate Kate saw a number of small cabins built against the sixteen-foot walls. Crude wooden signs nailed above the doors announced each cabin's purpose: Captain's Quarters, Store, Bunkhouse, Warehouse. Off to one side stood the Blacksmith Shop.

Trappers clad in dirty buckskin shirts, greasy cowhide breeches, and deerskin moccasins lounged about. In the chill of the morning, some even wore buffalo robes.

"Say, Missouri, how is ya?" Arkansas hollered to an acquaintance busily unloading a pallet of furs near the warehouse door. He was one of the few people doing anything.

Scores of Indians loitered around the fort, both inside and out.

"They're Shoshone, aren't they, Arkansas?" Kate asked, recognizing this tribe as the same Indians who had visited another part of the train earlier in the week.

"Yes, Ma'am," the trapper replied.

"They're not like the Sioux, are they?" Kate asked anxiously. The memories of the horse stealing and the bloody scalps were still fresh.

"No, little lady," he replied. "They're peaceful. Some folks call 'em Snakes, 'cuz they used to paint snake heads on sticks to scare their enemies—the Pawnee and such. More 'n likely the name's on account of them livin' near the Snake River."

The Shoshone looked like other Indians Kate had seen on the trail, except for one thing—their clothing was beautiful. The women's fringed skirts of deer and antelope skin were covered with intricate needlework, shimmering with hundreds of tiny colored beads. The men wore tanned hide vests in soft brown, which had been beaded with designs of teepees or warriors or animals.

Just then the trapper pointed Kate toward the general store. "I'm goin' to git some new horseshoes on Red, Miz Kate. I'll meet ya in jest a few minutes outside the store."

Kate felt uneasy about going to the fort's store by herself. She missed Mama and wished she were here to help her decide what to get. But Mama wasn't here, and Kate knew she would just have to manage. Setting her jaw, she headed for the store.

Just then a man's loud voice floated through an open cabin door to her right. The sign over the cabin read, "Captain's Quarters."

"I'm telling you, you can't make it past here with those wagons," boomed a voice, punctuated by the sound of a fist pounding on wood.

Kate peeked through the door and saw a man with long sideburns standing behind a large desk. A gilded picture of Queen Victoria hung on the log wall behind him. That must be Captain Grant, she thought.

"I believe we can, Captain. And more important, the people of this wagon train believe we can," said a voice she recognized as Dr. Whitman's.

"You couldn't even make it past Fort Boise with your own wagon when you came through in '36. Remember? What makes you think an entire train of wagons can get through?"

"This time it's different, Grant," the doctor said firmly. "I know the obstacles ahead, but we've got the manpower to overcome them this time— even with the wagons. I'm sure we can make it all the way to the Willamette Valley."

"I'm not really part of this argument, Doctor. I only contracted with you to guide the train this far. But I agree with Captain Grant; I think it's foolhardy. Even if your people do get through the Blues, what makes you think you can get five thousand head of cattle through there? You'll lose 'em in those mountains!"

"I'll tell you why we'll make it, John Gantt," said another voice. Kate edged closer to the doorway and saw that the voice belonged to Peter Burnett.

"We've overcome much to get this far—the lack of food, water, firewood; rough river crossings; alkali dust; the loss of animals—even the death of loved ones. Nothing has stopped us." He gestured behind him toward the river and the encamped emigrants. "Whatever lies ahead of us, we'll overcome that, too. We are determined to finish this journey, Gantt, and we *will* finish it!"

"That may be, Burnett, but we need supplies. Captain Grant here's scalping us with his prices. Fifty cents for a pint of sugar. Outrageous!" Kate didn't recognize this voice.

"It isn't just that, Nesmith." The legs of a hardback chair scraped on the wood floor. "You're holding back on us, Captain. Your store won't sell us enough, and you refuse to sell us any cattle to slaughter. Those of us heading toward California turn off here, and we can't get all the way out there without more provisions."

"I'd like to sell as much as I can, Mr. Childs, but I can't jeopardize the fort," the captain responded. "Winter's coming."

"Grant, either you sell us supplies or I'll have to—"

"Now, Childs," admonished Dr. Whitman, "Captain Grant has been as generous as possible. Let's not threaten him."

Kate's attention was suddenly diverted by a hand on her shoulder. She whipped around.

"Good morning, Kate." John Prentiss tipped his floppy hat to reveal his dark wavy hair.

"Hello, John." Kate could feel her face blushing.

"I've been sent on a mission to fetch you."

"About what?" Fear clawed at Kate's throat.

"Jane's looking for you."

"Is she all right?"

John's teeth flashed in a quick smile. "Other than butterflies in her stomach, I'm sure she's quite well," he said. "Vaughn has asked Mr. Mills for Jane's hand and he's agreed. The wedding is tomorrow before we leave. Jane needs your help."

The next day Reverend Garrison officiated at the wedding between Jane Mills and William Vaughn, held in a large meadow beside the south bank of the Snake River. When the emigrants resumed their journey the day after the ceremony, the newlyweds rolled forward in William's wagon to waves of blessing from all the others.

42

SALMON FALLS

Thursday–Saturday, August 31–September 9

The emigrants followed the Snake River for a week along a sun-broiled plateau of bristly sagebrush. The three-foot-high bushes made it difficult for the first five or six wagons in the column, but their oxen hooves and wheels crushed the sagebrush for the rest. The soil was dry and soft, and it was quickly churned into a fine powder that clogged wheels and filled worn out boots. Once again, the dust hung over the train, choking and blinding both people and animals. Even with a bandanna tied around her nose and mouth Kate still breathed in enough dust to develop a rasping cough that only went away when they stopped for the night. The poor unprotected animals were coughing all the time now.

The ever-changing beauty of the river helped a little to make up for the horrible dust. They came across places where thousands of years ago its torrents had sliced deep canyons through volcanic lava, creating perpendicular cliffs several hundred feet high. Camped on top of these cliffs, though, the emigrants were forced to lug water up to the top in buckets for themselves and their animals.

A few days after leaving Fort Hall, the emigrants encountered the panoramic American Falls, where they estimated that the river dropped about seventy-five feet over a distance of two hundred feet or more.

The Winfields stopped their team to watch the water explode downward, gushing and spouting, and bathing massive boulders. Splashing and playing, it formed foaming torrents through the glistening rocks, crafting channels of cold water that whipped up into dangerous rapids. Over the bottom of the falls hung a rainbow, shimmering in the early afternoon sun.

"Papa, I wish Mama could have been here to see this," Kate exclaimed. "She would have loved the rainbow."

Jacob nodded without taking his eyes off the scene. "Time to be movin' on," he said.

Four days later, after passing Twin Falls, where an enormous boulder split the river into two cascading waterfalls, they began to hear a distant roar up ahead.

"That's what we call Salmon Falls," Arkansas announced as he came by on his Appaloosa. "We're almost there."

A short while later Kate could easily see how this waterfall got its name. The Snake River descended about twenty-five feet over approximately three hundred yards of rocks and boulders that looked as though some giant had carelessly strewn them about. Rushing between the boulders, the river formed dozens of cold channels for hundreds of wild salmon, who jumped their way upstream. Wriggling and twirling, their long silvery bodies leaped through the spray and back into the water.

"Look, over there!" Jake spoke just above the waterfall's roar.

Two Indian men were sprawled on a huge rock beside one of the channels. One gripped a sharp elk horn spear.

"Where are their fishing poles?" Jake wondered aloud.

"Jes' watch," the mountain man suggested as he patted his horse's neck.

Without moving a muscle the copper skinned Indians waited for the right moment. Then, with a quick strike, one suddenly thrust his spear into the water. Within seconds a dripping salmon wriggled on its tip. Then the other one suddenly scooped a flopping fish out of the water with his bare hand. Kate was amazed.

"This tribe of Shoshone live mostly on salmon," Arkansas explained as Papa clucked the oxen back into motion. "They trade with it, too. You'll see in jest a few minutes."

Soon their wagon approached a small Indian village. Barefoot and half-naked children with stringy black hair huddled in groups playing in the dirt near huts of green willow brush. Some heavy set women, dressed in coats so bare Kate could see holes, were slicing fresh salmon and laying them on flat rocks to dry in the sun. Two dogs, whose rib cages poked through their thin skin, rummaged near some clumps of sagebrush. These Shoshone were very different from those Kate had seen at Fort Hall.

"These people are poor, Saw," Kate worried. "How do they survive in the winter?"

"Some of 'em starve, Miz Kate," Arkansas answered as he flipped open his leather saddlebag and tugged out a piece of almond colored cloth.

"I'm sure they don't actually starve, Kate," her father interjected, hoisting himself on the backboard to retrieve something from the wagon.

"But they do, Mr. Winfield," the mountain man answered. "They eat nuts and seeds, maybe some rabbit. Many of 'em don't make it through the winter."

"Someone should do something!" Kate turned her palms up in exclamation.

"Out here, winter's a hard time fer everyone, Miz Kate," Arkansas replied.

Just then, one of the braves, a man in tattered gray pants, approached Arkansas with two reed baskets full of fresh salmon. Scout sensed no danger and scampered up to him wagging his tale. Without a word Arkansas handed the Shoshone the cloth and took a bushel of salmon. Kate watched as Papa did the same thing with a wool shirt he had pulled out of the wagon. The Shoshone grunted something and softly padded away.

"Supper for everyone." Papa's voice broke the spell. "And enough salmon to get us to Fort Boise." Kate liked the idea of fresh fish, but the sight of those poor Indians haunted her for miles.

Thirty miles northwest of Salmon Falls, the Snake River channeled itself into a wide bay with two narrow islands in the middle. Arkansas had sent word that this was the place the Company would finally cross over to the river's north side. The wagons should follow the near bank until they were opposite the islands and then use them as stepping stones to the other side.

Kate and Jacob and Ole Joe spent the next day caulking the wagon and repacking their supplies. All day long memories of Mama flooded through Kate—she and her mother dipping their sticks in tar to waterproof the wagons before the Caw River crossing; the sound of Mama's voice when she talked to Papa; Mama in the pouring rain wedging the plank under the stuck wagon wheel; the smell of bubbling split pea soup in the iron kettle, and the taste of Mama's fresh warm cornbread.

Tears welled up in her eyes, but Kate couldn't cry. It had been almost four weeks since Mama's death, and she still hadn't been able to cry. She needed to cry, but the pain was so deep that it seemed to stifle the tears. The sense of loss was overwhelming; there were days when she missed her mother with each passing hour. But Mama was dead, and there was nothing she could do about it.

Nothing but grieve. But Kate didn't know how to grieve.

43

SNAKE RIVER CROSSING

Thursday, September 14

Early in the morning, just after sunrise, the Winfield wagon rumbled up to the water's edge. Behind them lay the steep hills through which they had come down to the bank at the narrowest portion of the river channel. Two shallow islands covered with grass lay in the middle of the river—"stepping stones" to the other side, as Papa called them.

Beyond the river stretched endless miles of sagebrush flatland, leading to the hazy morning outline of more mountains.

Slowly Papa and Joe guided their ox team down into the river toward the first island, about a hundred yards away. Kate could see Jake perched in the wagon behind his father and Ole Joe, holding on to Scout, with Eli and Tess following behind. Kate rode Midnight deeper into the muddy river, and he carefully felt his way over the unfamiliar bottom. The water was up well over the horse's knees now, and its dank smell rose up to her. As more teams and wagons entered the river, the sounds of men hollering and oxen baying filled the air. On the far bank some cranes ignored the commotion and continued scratching the sand for breakfast.

It wasn't long before they reached the first island and then promptly forded another narrow channel over to the second island.

Here, however, things got difficult. The current between the second island and the far bank was much stronger than it had been for the first two crossings.

"Joe, we'll rope our wagon behind the Applegates, and eight others will tie up behind us," Papa called out, dumping water out of his boot. "Everybody's crossing this way and even putting some of the heavier wagons side by side. With those men on the far bank hauling on the ropes tied to the front wagon we should be able to avoid being swept downriver by the current."

"Kate, you stay here with Jake and Tess. I'll come back for you," Papa said. "And keep Scout out of the way."

Kate let Tess munch on some nearby grass while Jake held Scout, and they watched the scene unfold in front of them. When all ten wagons were roped together, Jacob and Joe mounted the driver's seat. Just then Dr. Whitman rode up with three other men.

"We'll ride beside your team and try to keep it steady, Jacob," Dr. Whitman offered, pushing his sleeves up to his elbow. The doctor nudged his dripping Paint to the left side of the wagon. "Some of the weaker animals have already had trouble with this current. We'll try to keep your team from getting swept down."

With that Papa clucked the six-oxen team into motion. Slowly Caleb and Joshua and the others plodded down the soft river bank, their big hooves leaving deep imprints in the mud. Burdened with the weight of the heavy wagon, the animals lumbered steadily ahead, their massive bodies pushing against the water's current. The tin pans and wooden buckets clattered and clanged against the wagon with each step forward.

Kate could hear the men on the opposite bank now encouraging one another. "Heave!" they yelled as they pulled on the heavy ropes tied to the Applegates' wagon. "Take up the slack! Keep it tight!"

She could see the water churning at their wagon, higher and higher, almost spilling into the wagon bed.

Then, all of a sudden, Caleb's head sank under the water, and he almost disappeared. He had stumbled into a hole! Immediately one of the riders grabbed the ox's horn and pulled him back out. The frightened ox surfaced, hawing loudly for air.

Before Kate could take a breath, the horse of one of the riders abruptly stumbled in the wild current, losing its footing and plunging down. Instantly Dr. Whitman wheeled his Paint around and grabbed the horse by its bridle. "Let go of the reins!" the doctor screamed to the rider as he dragged the terrified animal toward the far shore.

By noon Kate and Jake and the Winfield cattle had reached the far shore, too.

"Glad to see you made it!" Kate recognized John's voice. She twirled around to see his Palomino's gold coat glistening from the water.

"Have you finished helping everybody across?" Kate asked, retying her bonnet under her chin.

"Almost. But we're having some trouble. Eyers, mostly. Thinks he can drive his mules over by himself."

Kate glanced at the island across the last channel. Sure enough, the portly Englishman was flailing his fat arms in the air trying to make a point to someone. Near some juniper trees and hitched to his four mules was his family's covered wagon, piled high with their belongings.

"Where's his family?" Kate asked.

"They're already here. The old coot was being so stubborn that they begged to go on across with the Rubys. They're waiting for him."

A short while later, while Kate and Jake were repacking the big wagon along the riverbank, they heard the sound of the Eyers's mules braying and hawing. Kate and her brother watched as Eyers drove the wagon down the bank and into the water. They could see his whip flying through the air as he forced them onward.

Within minutes the swift current was sweeping the mules and the wagon helplessly downstream. Frantically the mules twisted in their harnesses, turning upstream and scrambling for sure footing in the mud. Kate could hear the man screaming at his team, but it was to no avail. They had panicked in the current, and their thrashing overturned the wagon, throwing Eyers into the river. Unable to get out of their harnesses and held down by the heavy wagon that was now sinking, the mules began to drown. Before she knew it, Mr. Eyers himself had disappeared from sight, sucked under by the relentless river.

Yelling men rode out into the river, trying to find the mules or the wagon or Eyers—something to haul to safety. But there was nothing. The river had swallowed all of them, without a trace. The current resumed its swift journey downstream as if nothing had happened.

"Serves him right," Jake announced, after it was all over.

"Jake, don't say such a thing," Kate admonished her brother with a glare. "Nobody deserves to die like that."

"But he was mean."

"He was human, Jake, with faults just like all of us."

Kate surprised herself. She sounded just like her mother.

"And besides, look." She pointed down the shore. "He left a wife and children."

There, standing on the bank, their hands over their faces, wailing loudly in despair, were Eyers's wife and a young son and daughter. In an instant they had lost a husband and father and all their provisions and possessions.

A man as stubborn as Eyers can die quickly in this wilderness, Kate thought.

44

FORGIVEN

Monday, September 18

For the last several days, after filling up the water barrels at the Snake River, the company of emigrants had trekked across a waterless, flat, and dusty landscape to reach the green banks of the Boise where they had camped.

The mood of the emigrants was not good. Everyone was cranky and tired and growing increasingly anxious about crossing the Blue Mountains—an ordeal that lay not many days ahead of them. Tempers were flaring. Yesterday a fight had broken out in another camp, and the day before a man had actually stabbed someone. Husbands could be heard ordering their wives around and yelling at their children. Children scuffled at the smallest provocation, and dog fights were breaking out more frequently. Even the cattle seemed ill at ease.

Just tonight, Kate thought with a scowl, the tension had infected their family. While Jake had been helping Joe lift the yoke off Caleb and Joshua for the night, he had asked Kate, "What's for supper?"

"Beans," she had replied, heaving a food sack off the wagon and shaking off its dust.

"Again? Papa, I'm tired of beans," he had whined as he set the yoke near the trunk of a juniper tree.

"Jake, stop the whining. We're low on supplies and don't have much choice." Papa had clutched his jacket around him against the falling late afternoon temperature.

"Why didn't we buy more food at the last fort?" With puckered lips, Jake had persisted.

"Jake, be quiet!" Kate had ordered. "And fetch me some water from the river," she had added wearily, taking the two empty water buckets out of the wagon.

"I don't have to do what you say," he had countered, planting his grimy bare feet in the dirt, his equally grimy hands on his hips. "You're always telling me what to do now that Mama's gone. You're not Mama, and I don't have to listen to you."

"Jake!" The tone of Papa's rebuke had been sharp. "Your sister knows she isn't your mother, but she's the only woman with us men. She can't do it alone. Now go and fetch the water."

Without a word, the boy had marched toward the river, a bucket in each hand.

As she watched her brother go, the weariness inside Kate had become overwhelming. Somehow she had gotten through the meal and cleaned up the dishes, but when Jake went to play with the Applegate boys and Papa went to look in on Catherine Stevenson, she had come down to the river to be by herself.

It wasn't just that she had resented her brother's whining; she knew that she was totally exhausted. Kate also knew that it wasn't as much the physical toll that the heat and the dust and the walking were taking on her. It was an exhaustion of soul, one that had been growing in her ever since her mother's death.

Kate found a grassy spot and sat down against a juniper tree, wondering if she had ever felt more tired. Scout lay down beside her and soon dozed off, his chin on his front paws. In the softly fading light of evening she watched the dark water hurry past, while the ever-present wind brought to her ears the whoo—oo—oo—oo call of mourning doves. *It is so peaceful here,* she thought. *But we can't stay long—it will be dark soon.*

Suddenly, the whoo—oo—oo—oo of a mourning dove sounded very near. Kate looked up to find the light gray and brown bird sitting in a bush about ten feet away. *It looks just like the ones back home,* she thought. The dove was looking straight at her. And once again it gave its mournful call.

A memory flashed into Kate's mind: She and her mother used to throw bread crumbs to mourning doves in the yard of their house.

"Mama," Kate whispered. "How much I miss you! I can't take your place—I can't take care of Papa and Jake. I don't know how to give them everything they need.

"I didn't know how to help you, either, Mama. Please forgive me. I tried everything, Mama. I didn't know what else to do. I didn't mean to let you die. Oh, Mama, I didn't *want* you to die!"

There it was! Kate had finally blurted out the guilt of her mother's death. Kate had believed that her mother's death was her fault—that somehow if she had tried other herbs, or diagnosed the symptoms earlier, or done *something*, then her mother wouldn't have died.

With a strangled cry from the bottom of her heart, Kate began to sob openly. Weeks of pent-up tears flooded her cheeks as she cried out all her pain and guilt with her shoulders heaving. Scout came over to her and put his head in her lap, as if he knew what she was feeling and wanted to comfort her.

Just then the mourning dove flew out of the bush and landed right in front of Kate. Cocking its head to one side, it softly cooed a few times, its eyes fixed on her, as if it had a message for her. Scout raised his head and looked at the bird but didn't move.

Drying her eyes with her hands, Kate whispered, "Mama, did you ask God to send this bird to me?"

And then, very clearly, she heard Dr. Whitman's voice in her heart.

"Kate, you did everything I would've done. There was nothing more you could do; there was nothing anyone could do."

This time his words washed over her like a welcome rain, and she began to cry again. But now they were tears of relief and healing. That was why the mourning dove had come—to tell her that Mama's death wasn't her fault. She had done everything anyone could have done.

Kate felt forgiven.

By her mother and by God and—by herself.

All at once the mourning dove flew off across the river into the gathering night, giving its mournful call, whoo—oo—oo—oo.

"Come on, Scout," Kate said with a much lighter heart. "Let's get back to camp. They'll be wondering where we've been."

45

FORT BOISE

Wednesday–Sunday, September 20–24

The emigrants had followed the Boise River until it joined the Snake, and there they had come to Fort Boise. The fort was the result of an old fur trade rivalry between the Americans and the British. After Wyeth built Fort Hall in 1834, the British Hudson Bay Company had ordered Fort Boise to be constructed to compete with him. Now both forts were British, far-flung outposts of the mighty British Empire.

This is the least impressive of all the forts we have visited so far, Kate thought to herself. Its fifteen-foot-high pole stockade enclosed an area only about one hundred feet square. The British flag flopped in the breeze. Greasy-haired Shoshone Indians, wrapped in blankets so dirty they had lost their patterns, milled around outside the gray adobe walls with nothing to do. A misspelled sign, "General Warhouse," painted on two slats nailed together, swung over an adobe building that leaned slightly to one side.

As Kate pushed open the rickety door to the store, she saw a rusty iron double pulley hanging next to a scythe and three shovels. A barrel of gunpowder sat next to a wooden box labeled "Irish Soap." The shelving behind the counter contained colored bottles of all shapes and sizes, some full and others half empty. She could smell the stale tobacco from the earthenware jar that was still open on the counter.

"What can I do for you folks?" the storekeeper asked, scratching his bald head and leaving a smudge of soot from the stove.

"Got any flour or bacon?" Jacob asked, picking up a bottle labeled West India Stomach Bitters. Kate recognized this medicine, made in Missouri, that was reported to cure a person's ailments. Mama always steered clear of such "quackery," as she called it.

"Can't say as I do," the clerk replied. "Fact is, I had quite a bit of corn-meal but I've done sold all of that to them that got here earlier today. Been out of flour now for weeks. Ain't got no rice or sugar, neither. Guess you folks are plumb out of luck."

On the way back to their wagon, Papa commented to Kate, "They're not any more ready for all of us than Fort Hall was."

Without any fresh supplies, the Company had re-crossed the Snake River and then bounced northwest across the arid sagebrush hills about twelve miles to another river, called the Malheur. This one had guided them twenty-two miles back to the Snake, where they had encamped early Wednesday at a wide curve in the river Dr. Whitman called Farewell Bend. Surrounded by parched foothills of burnt sienna, this was the place where they would leave the river for the last time.

It wasn't long before Warren Applegate appeared at the Winfields' covered wagon.

"Mr. Winfield, sir, can you help my Papa?" he panted. "We lost our ox, ole Betsy, a little while ago. She just couldn't take it anymore." Warren's dark eyes were sad. "Papa wants to dress up the meat, but it's hot and he's got to do it right away. He sent me to get you and Joe."

"Can I come, too?" Jake asked.

"A boy's got to learn sometime, I guess," Jacob replied. The top of the jockey box jostled as Kate's father opened it for his knife. "I'm going to stop by Mrs. Stevenson's afterward, Kate, and help her with that back tire that's giving her trouble. Then Joe and I will be at Applegate's camp. We should be back by supper."

A short while later, with Scout trotting along just ahead, Kate skirted scruffy green juniper trees and strolled down to the water's edge. The afternoon seemed quiet. The wispy clouds overhead had almost disappeared in the heat of the day, leaving a wide expanse of blue as far as she could see. The river at the bend mirrored the surrounding sand hill peaks and valleys almost perfectly, as if someone had painted on it. To the north it curled lazily around the hills and then disappeared. The surface of the water was calm today, but Kate knew that the undercurrents in this river could suck a man down in a heartbeat. She had watched it happen.

She put her arms in the warm water near the bank. The palms of her hands felt crusty and calloused; she couldn't remember when they had felt really clean. Each day that they traveled the trail, dust got into every crevice of her skin, and in spite of washing whenever she could, she wondered if she'd ever be truly clean again.

Behind her the wagon bonnets that had once gleamed white in the sun now appeared dirty and had been patched many times. Wagon beds once painted bright greens and blues were faded and bore the gouges and scratches of months of hardships. The cows grazing on the short grass looked thinner, and the few chickens that were left didn't cluck as much.

"You're a good dog, Scout," she said aloud as she found a rock on which to sit for awhile. Scout's moist tongue felt rough on her hand. Kate ruffled the dog's tan ears, tangled from too many dusty days on the trail without a combing. It seemed like a lifetime ago when she had found him being whipped by that evil man. So much had happened, and they had come so far—more than fifteen hundred miles from Independence, Papa had said. They were in the last stretch now. Some hard days lay ahead, Dr. Whitman had said, but they were now only 175 miles from his mission.

After an hour or so at the river, Kate rose, stretched her thin frame, and headed back to camp. When suppertime neared and the men had still not returned, Kate decided to go and find them. Threading her way through the shrubs toward the Applegates' wagons, she heard laughter. Kate recognized the voices of the boys, Jake and the twins. Through the branches of a juniper, she spotted the Applegate twins and Jake standing in front of a dead ox with a bloated stomach.

"That was a good one." Joshua Applegate rubbed his forehead with one hand. "That's the biggest stomach I've ever seen."

"The hot weather made it swell really fast," Warren added, tugging off his second boot. "It's as big as a barrel. You gonna try, Jake?"

"I don't want to bounce my head against some slimy ole ox stomach." Jake made a face.

"Just try it, Jake. It's fun." Warren backed up and wriggled his bare toes in the sand. "Like this."

With that, the youngster lowered his head and charged at the ox's stomach as if he'd been shot out of a slingshot. When his head hit the elastic pouch, he bounced back at least six feet.

"Bet you can't do better than that!" He stood up, raising his arms like a prizefighter who had just won the fight.

Jake squared his jaw and popped out his suspenders. "Can too," he retorted, in a sudden change of mind. "I can even do better!"

With his hands balled into tight fists, Jake backed up farther than both the twins. The boy scraped the toes of his bare feet in the warm sand like a mad bull and arched his shoulders. Then, eyeing his prey and pursing his lips, he sucked in a couple of deep breaths.

"Charge!" he yelled.

And with that, he took off, running at full speed toward dead ox. At the last second he launched himself through the air and landed headfirst on the pouch. But . . . he didn't bounce back!

Kate gulped and almost swallowed a gnat. Jake had hit the ox's stomach so hard that his head was actually stuck inside it!

"Help! Somebody get him out!" Warren started yelling. "His head's stuck!"

Kate darted from behind the shrub and grabbed her brother's left leg while Warren clutched at his right, and Joshua tugged on his belt.

They pulled and pulled.

Jake struggled and struggled.

Finally Jake's head popped out with a big *phoosh!* Everyone dropped onto the ground, laughing.

Everyone that is except Jake.

The story of his escapade with the ox's stomach quickly made the rounds, for when Dr. Whitman returned from visiting William and Jane Vaughn that evening, he had already heard the tale. Jake was the topic of conversation throughout the Company. At supper Jake maintained that his head hurt and that he wasn't hungry, so he crawled into the pup tent just as the stars were emerging in a deepening black sky.

"Looks like the lad may have a future in bull fighting," Whitman chuckled as his fork scraped a last bite of beans.

"I wouldn't be surprised, Doctor." Jacob shook his head in disbelief. "He might need to brush up on his delivery though."

"I think he'll be thinkin' on things fer awhile," Joe smiled. "Saw the Applegate twins washin' their heads after it happened. Maybe he'll feel better tomorrow."

"Speaking of tomorrow," the doctor changed the subject, "I'm going on home in the morning, Jacob. My wife has sent word that she's having a bit of trouble with the Indians. I'll meet you at the mission." The legs of the cane-back chair seemed to creak even more tonight when the doctor rocked forward to set his empty plate on the ground.

"I'll send one of our Cayuse guides, a man named Stickus, who'll pilot you the rest of the way. He'll probably meet you in the Blue Mountains.

In the meantime don't let anyone convince you to stay on this river. The country up north there is impassable."

The next morning, with some foreboding, the Winfields bade farewell to Dr. Whitman and to the river. Ahead lay the most difficult part of the journey.

49

BURNT RIVER CANYON

Monday–Sunday, September 25–October 1

The Oregon Emigration Company had faced difficult terrain in the miles since Independence: they had forded swift and dangerous rivers and had lowered the wagons down the nearly vertical slope of Windlass Hill. But nothing could have prepared them for the rough country they encountered after leaving Farewell Bend.

"Joe!" Jacob yelled, stopping the team a few yards up a steep slope. "We're gonna have to double team again. Go ask Jesse Applegate for the loan of two of his oxen again—it'll take more than six of ours to haul our wagon out of this ravine."

Kate sighed. This was the second time this morning that they had been forced to do this. The company was following the narrow Burnt River through a twisting and turning canyon whose sides were steep rocky slopes cut by deep ravines. There was no discernible road up and down the ravines that cut through the slopes down to the river, so they had to repeatedly cross and re-cross the stream to find passage for the wagons.

But the worst part was that the gullies and ravines were so steep that the usual number of oxen used to pull the wagons was not enough. In order to haul the wagons up and out of the gullies the men had to double team the wagons, hitching and unhitching the oxen and mules. Going down the steep slopes, they had to attach chain locks to the wheels and haul back on ropes to keep the wagons from sliding down into the ravines. Sweating in the hot sun, they then had to use the ropes again to help the oxen pull the wagons up out of the ravines. Progress was agonizingly slow. Kate guessed that they hadn't made two miles in the four hours since the nooning.

"Saw, this is the worst country I've ever seen," Jacob complained to the mountain man when Arkansas rode by on his Appaloosa. Kate had heard her father grumbling to himself and Joe for the last hour or so.

"Arkansas, why is it called the Burnt River Canyon?" she asked, rummaging in the supply wagon for something to tie one of her tattered boots together.

"'Cuz of all the fires in these parts," the mountain man explained, letting his Appaloosa's reins slacken for a moment.

"Why so many fires?" Kate persisted.

"Lightning strikes, I reckon, Miss."

The land took its toll. Wagons flipped over on the steep slopes. Shrunken wagon wheels popped out of their iron rims. Axles snapped with the strain. Oxen languished and died, unable to bear the heat or the weight any longer. Cowhide boots wore out, and many emigrants started walking barefoot.

Finally, after three days and twenty-five miles of toil the emigrants struggled up the last hill out of the canyon and beheld a scene that soothed their weary souls. In front of them stretched a ten-mile-wide plain of sagebrush and grass-bordered rivers, surrounded by mountains of thick pine forests capped in shining white snow. Over the tops of the mountains were heaped piles of fluffy white clouds, the sun splashing rays of light through them on the slopes below. Thirty miles away to the northeast loomed a chain of ridges whose cool blue haze announced their name—the Blue Mountains.

"Mistah Jacob, I seen Mistah Burnett this mornin' when I checked on our cattle," Joe offered on Wednesday as he steered the lead oxen around another clump of dry sagebrush. "He told me to tell ya that we're gonna camp by the tree."

"What tree?" Kate asked, wiping the perspiration off her face with the hem of her apron.

"Seems there's a tree out here all by itself," Joe replied, whisking his floppy hat off his white head and wiping the sweat off his brow. "Arkansas says it's been here forever. Calls it the Lonesome Pine."

Jake was the first to spot it. "Could that bush way up there be the tree?"

As they trekked slowly across the plain, the bush seemed to grow until it was transformed into a tall slender pine tree, taller even than their barn roof back home. By Friday afternoon, the Winfields' company was circling their wagons near it.

"How did it get way out here?" Jake had asked, tugging off his floppy hat so he could see up to the top.

"No one knows," Arkansas replied from his Appaloosa. "Always been a landmark for us guides and the fur traders. It's a brave ole thing, out here all by its lonesome. That's why we call it the Lonesome Pine."

The next afternoon while they were trudging north, Jake glanced back.

"Papa," he piped up. "Where's the tree?"

Kate whirled round in the dust, snagging her skirt on a sage bush. The tree had mysteriously vanished! Later that evening, after they camped, they learned the sad truth: one of the emigrants behind them had felled the pine for firewood and hadn't even burned it, because the wood was too green.

After centuries of guarding the plain, the old tree was gone. "You have to wonder whether that's a sign of the changes to come," Papa had commented sadly during supper. Kate was afraid that Papa might just be right about that.

By Saturday the emigrants had trailed into a valley that was so beautiful Kate caught her breath and wondered if she were dreaming. Called the Grande Ronde, this basin in front of the lofty Blue Mountains was rich in giant pines and succulent grasses, and crossed by rushing streams full of trout and larch. At the camps that night some of the emigrants talked about settling down there, but realized that they would be so far away from the settlements in the Willamette Valley that life in that heavenly spot would be impractical.

Sadly, as if they were being warned that mortal dangers lay ahead, the emigrants lost Mrs. Ruby, the woman who helped the Eyers family across the Snake River. She died of a fever and was buried there on the first of October.

50

THE BLUE MOUNTAINS

Monday, October 2

Early this morning the Winfield wagon was among the first to begin the ascent into the dreaded Blue Mountains, the last mountain range the weary travelers would have to cross before reaching their destinations in the Oregon Territory.

Spruce and pine trees were so thick on the slope that Kate could hardly see Ole Joe, who was only ten feet away. Behind their wagon, dozens of other canvas covered wagons followed in single file. The sound of cattle lowing in the valley behind them echoed up through the forest.

"They're so big!" Jake marveled at the sheer size of the ponderosa pines in front of them. "It takes three looks to see to the top!" Her brother was right. The reddish bark of the pine extended at least two hundred feet up and at least five or six feet in diameter. Kate craned her neck and held onto the top of her bonnet.

A few yards in front of them, at the head of the wagon column, Papa stood looking at the forest, his hat in one hand and an ax in the other. Peter Burnett and Lindsey Applegate joined him, along with Arkansas.

"No way around these mountains, is there Arkansas?" Burnette asked, frowning at the thick forest.

"Nope. And the trees is as thick every place else as they are here. Reckon we're gonna have to cut a road for these wagons right here," the mountain man responded.

"Well, there's nothin' for it 'cept to get busy with the axes," Papa said, hoisting his ax up on one shoulder.

"I'll pass the word down the line for every man that can swing an ax to join us up here," Jesse Applegate volunteered and turned to walk back down the line of wagons.

Joe threw a worried look at Jacob as they walked back to the jockey box to fetch their axes. "Mistah Jacob, our axes are right dull!"

"I know, Joe. Everyone else's is, too. We'll just have to do the best we can."

Kate wondered how they would ever do it. Unfortunately no one had been able to sharpen axes since before they left Independence, and the trees were thick up ahead for as far as she could see.

Before long about forty of the able-bodied men hiked up to the front of the company with their axes and got to work. Groups of two or three men would attack each tree, cutting notches into the trunk as the chips flew. The *thwock, thwock, thwock* of their axes biting into the thick trunks of the fir trees resounded through the forest—blow after blow, hour after hour.

Once trees were down, men would drag them far enough out of the way with ropes so that the wagons could move ahead for a few yards over the jagged stumps.

While the husbands and fathers were busy felling the trees, it fell to Kate and the other women to carefully guide the ox teams through the narrow passageway opened up by their men. Often the space between the trees was so tight that the hubs of the wheels left scars on the trunks as they passed.

"Thank you, Kate," Papa said as he plopped down on a felled spruce tree with a tin cup in his hand. Kate ladled water into the cup from a bucket Jake was holding, as Scout came up to Jacob wagging his tail. Papa guzzled down the water in three swallows.

"This is taking a dreadful long time. By the time we have to make camp tonight I don't think the last wagon will have started up the hill," he sighed.

All the men's shirts were soaked through with sweat, showing how hard they were working.

"Do you think we'll ever get through all this, Mr. Prentiss?" Jake asked, as Kate scooped more water into John's tin cup.

"Someday, Jake," John replied before taking a sip. "But it's going dreadful slow. Six trees in four hours, and it's almost noon. At this rate it might be the dead of winter before we get out of here."

Kate smiled at him. "I have every confidence in you men," she declared. "You can get us through this—with some help from the Almighty."

Ever since that day at Farewell Bend and her experience with the mourning dove, Kate had felt a renewed sense of hope about life. She now believed that God had sent the dove to comfort her and to let her know that He was watching over her and would take care of her.

John swigged his last drop of water. "Well, Kate, it sounds like we're both praying for the same thing," he observed with a smile.

"We are indeed, John." She smiled back at him.

Kate missed her mother greatly and was reminded of her by everything from the blue wildflowers in the Grand Ronde Valley to the smell of trail bread over a fire. But, although she didn't understand why God had let her mother die and was still angry at Him about it, her trust in His mercy and goodness was starting to grow.

Her thoughts were interrupted by the approach of a lone rider—an Indian with a single feather poking out from the back of his long wavy black hair. His smoky buckskin shirt had fringe on the shoulders and sleeves, and beads dangled on buckskin ties at his chest and on his moccasins at the horse's belly.

But the new arrival's horse made an even stronger impression on Kate. With a deep mahogany body, its thick black mane and tail were tightly braided as if it was going to a horse show. The white spot on its forehead matched the white on its knees.

Arkansas stood up, burying the blade of his ax into the downed tree, and went to meet the Indian. "We've been waiting for you," he said to him, making signs with his hands and gesturing toward the seated men.

"I want ya to meet yer guide, gentlemen," the mountain man said to the group. "This is Stickus." Arkansas pointed to the Indian that Dr. Whitman had sent. "He knows these parts like the back of his hand."

"Kate," Jake whispered, tugging at Kate's sleeve. "Do you think he scalps people?"

Today her brother's question didn't bother her. She smiled. "If the doctor sent him, Jake, I'm sure he's peaceful."

The men gathered around the Indian.

"Does he speak English?" Peter Burnett asked.

"Not a word," Arkansas replied. "But he knows what we want and he's pretty good 'bout sign language."

Instantly Kate remembered her experience with the two Caw Indians. Sign language was universal.

While Arkansas was signing information to Stickus about the wagon train, Warren Applegate ran up to his father, all out of breath. "Papa, one of them cattle guards told me to tell you and Mr. Burnett that with so many men gone up here the cattle are wanderin' off and gettin' lost in the woods." Kate suddenly remembered John Gantt's words about this at Fort Laramie.

A short while later, as the men were getting back to work cutting down trees, Kate heard Papa give Jake an order. "Go down and check on our cattle. Make sure they're all there."

Jake jumped up and headed down the slope past the line of wagons. "Cattle Recovery Mission underway, Papa!" he yelled as he ran through the fallen pine needles. "If they're down there, I'll find 'em!"

Fortunately Jake did find the Winfields' remaining forty head of cattle huddled at the foot of the slope. Other families were not so fortunate. While the men cut down trees, dozens of women and children hunted for stray cows in the forest, their calls to one another echoing through the trees. The trees grew so close together that it was almost impossible to spot the cows, especially when they chose to lie down.

As the daylight faded in the forest the sounds of chopping gradually stopped, and the men shouldered their axes and wearily headed back to their wagons.

After supper Kate was washing off tin plates when John stopped to visit.

"Would you like some coffee?" Kate lifted the kettle from the edge of the fire and poured him a cup.

"Thanks, Kate," said John gratefully, sitting down on a felled tree trunk, his shoulders slumped with fatigue. "Not much progress today." John spoke between sips. "Only a few hundred yards. Every muscle in my body is sore. But I'm guessing we've got three or four more days of chopping before we get out of these trees."

"Maybe it'll go faster tomorrow," Kate remarked, trying to encourage him.

"Doesn't look like it. We've barely moved from where we camped last night."

After a short silence Kate spoke up. "John, something's been bothering me." She sat down beside him. "I wish I could help the Campbells."

"What's happening with the Campbells?" John swallowed the last of his coffee.

"I heard this afternoon that their seven-year-old son Lee died last night with a fever. They tried every remedy they knew, but his fever just wouldn't come down."

"I'm sorry to hear that, Kate," John replied, standing up to stretch his legs.

"I wish Dr. Whitman had been there," she went on sadly. "It's another loss. And that's what worries me."

"What do you mean?"

"Two people in just three days. Both with fevers."

"And Mr. Barlow, too," Jake interjected, dropping some firewood next to the fire.

"Mr. Barlow?" Kate and John chimed in together.

"Yep," Jake responded. "Warren told me that he died last night."

"Jackson Barlow?" John frowned. "That's three within three days, Kate."

Fear began nagging at Kate's heart.

51

FEVER

Wednesday, October 4

Early Wednesday morning Papa sent Kate down the line of wagons to check on the herd again. The smells of the forest were becoming familiar to her now. The fragrance of the spruce and pine trees hung in the crisp mountain air. The emigrants were responsible for some new smells—the aroma of fresh bark from yesterday's felled trees and the rancid odor of a night-visiting skunk that had been surprised by one of the company's dogs. Smoke from the breakfast fires mingled with the morning's mist in the upper branches of the trees.

With the loose sole of her boot still giving her trouble, Kate lifted her long skirt over a protruding root. Weeks of nettlesome sagebrush had ripped her petticoat into shreds along the bottom ruffle. She felt grimy this morning and longed for a bath.

More than that, however, Kate wished she had some clean clothes to wear. A bustle dress with a crocheted collar and a gathered skirt with a new petticoat to go with it would sure be nice. She wondered if she would ever again have a pair of shiny shoes with satin ribbons.

Lost in her thoughts, Kate nearly missed the sound of her name.

"Kate!" The voice was low and sounded weak. "Kate . . . Winfield!"

By the side of a wagon a man in a bleached-muslin shirt and striped trousers lay in the open on top of a thin bedroll. Behind the man's curly mustache his face was flushed, and his receding hair looked damp. Kate recognized Jeremiah Atkins.

"My head's hurting something fierce, Miss Winfield," Atkins managed to stammer. "Any chance you've got something with you?"

"May I feel your forehead?" Kate asked, anxiety rising up inside her.

The man was burning up with fever!

Now fear began rising in Kate's throat. Another fever. The fourth in four days—or at least, the fourth she knew about. Could there be more? Her heart began pounding inside her chest. What was going on?

"Mr. Atkins, I'll have to go back up to our wagon to get something. Will you be all right until I return?"

The man cradled his head in an elbow and moaned.

As Kate ran through the forest back up to their wagon, thoughts raced through her mind. Headaches. Fever. Moaning. Her mother had these symptoms. Was it *cholera*?

Ole Joe met her before their wagon came into view. "Miz Kate, yer Papa sent me to fetch ya."

The drawn out hissing screams of two nearby barn owls ghosted through the forest.

"Mr. Jake is feelin' poorly."

"What's wrong with him, Joe?" Afraid she already knew the answer, Kate tried to catch her breath from her fast climb.

"Says he's cold and his head hurts. His legs are achin' somethin' fierce. I put 'im in the wagon."

By that afternoon, reports of other sick people had reached the front of the train.

As John was trudging past their wagon on his way back up to chop trees, he called out to Kate:

"Seems like the whole train is getting sick, Kate. I just heard that another person is sick with a fever down in the valley."

Kate hopped off the big wagon's backboard. "I don't know what to do, John," she replied, picking up Mama's medical book from the chair. "The symptoms I'm hearing about are all the same. Headaches. Fever. Muscle aches."

"Any ideas?" John asked.

Kate flipped open the book. "The symptoms are the same as Mama's," Kate's voice quavered. "I've been thinking it must be cholera except for one thing. Jake's got a rash."

"Jake?" John rested the handle of his ax against the wagon tongue. "Where is he?"

"Inside the wagon. He's pretty sick."

John peered inside. "How're you doing, my friend?" His words were muffled through the wagon's bonnet. The *thwock, thwock, thwock* of axes in the distance was all Kate could hear.

When John emerged, his face was as white as if it had been starched.

"What's wrong?" Kate asked, closing the book on her lap.

"I think I know what this is."

Kate didn't like the somber tone in John's voice.

"It's not cholera, Kate, but it's just as bad. I think it's typhus."

"Typhus?" Kate's mind whirled like a leaf in the wind. What little she knew about typhus was that it was also highly contagious and could kill many people. Its symptoms were similar to cholera, including fever and chills.

"My parents died of typhus when I was twelve. They had that same rash. Come on, we've got to tell your Papa."

Leaving Scout with Jake and the wagon, Kate and John hiked up the steep incline to talk with her father. The sounds of axes biting into trees and men yelling directions grew louder. They found Joe and Jacob standing over a newly felled tree.

"Papa, we've got to talk with you." Kate was out of breath.

"How's Jake?" he asked, the veins on the top of both hands bulging from his grip on the wooden handle.

"No better, I'm afraid." Kate went on quickly. "Papa, John thinks he knows what this is, and if he's right, we're in serious trouble."

Jacob listened to the two of them and then said, "Kate, you go on back to Jake. I'm going to call an emergency council meeting for tonight."

"Jacob, I think Kate should be there," John suggested.

Jacob's face looked puzzled. "Why?" he asked.

"Because if this really is typhus, we're going to need her help."

52

THE MEETING

Wednesday Evening, October 4

That evening the Oregon Trail Emigrating Company held a Council meeting for the first time in many weeks. They convened in the forest near the Applegates' big wagon, which was just behind the Winfields', in a torch-lit clearing.

Kate stood next to her father and John, watching the men, and was struck by the changes in these men from the time they had gathered to vote that day back on the prairie. They were tired men now, with dark circles under their eyes and slumping shoulders. Dingy shirts and patched breeches evidenced miles of wear and tear. Hair fell in greasy ringlets or flattened bangs under floppy hats that had holes in them. Some of the men were barefoot.

"We can't let a little sickness stop us," Mr. Burnett was asserting.

"More than a few people are sick now, Peter," Jesse Applegate countered, standing next to him. "Even my nephew, Warren. We can't just leave them behind."

"We shouldn't travel until the sick are better," Mr. Lenox expressed his opinion. "My little Elizabeth isn't feeling well right now, but we don't know what it is."

"What about the snow?" Lancefield Johnson remarked, leaning against the trunk of a pine tree. "Has anyone looked at the clouds recently? If we were back east, I'd say they were snow clouds."

Kate buttoned her linen jacket against the evening chill, hoping that Mr. Johnson was wrong. Aside from their quilt and blankets, this was all she had to shield herself from the cold. And snow certainly wouldn't help those who were sick.

"Gentlemen!" Lindsey Applegate's voice got everyone's attention. "Jacob has called this meeting, so I'm going to hand it over to him. Jacob?"

Papa buttoned his leather vest over his shirt as if it would help him think better. "As you know," he started, "a number of people have gotten sick over the past few days. And we've had two people die."

"Make that three," Mr. Lenox interrupted, his voice grim. "I just learned that Mrs. Blevens passed away this afternoon."

The murmuring of the crowd was silenced only when Papa began speaking again.

"My daughter and John think they know what is going on. If they're right, we've got some serious decisions to make. John, please tell them what you told me."

"I'd like to have Kate speak first if I may. She's the one who first connected the illnesses."

Suddenly Kate felt very much on the spot. Every male eye had riveted toward her. She swallowed hard and stood up, tugging her jacket back down toward her waist.

"Gentlemen," she began. "Whatever this is, it is highly contagious. Far too many people have the same symptoms: headaches, fever, chills—"

"Lots of illnesses have those symptoms," one man interrupted her rudely. "That doesn't mean we have an epidemic on our hands."

"He's right, Jacob. We should take this slow. A few people getting sick doesn't mean we're in trouble," announced another.

The muttering grew louder, leaving Kate feeling awkward and isolated. But John's voice quieted everyone down.

"Gentlemen! We need to listen to Miss Winfield," he intoned strongly and firmly. "I've seen this before. These are the exact symptoms of the typhus that swept through Philadelphia back in '37. Hundreds of people died, including my parents. These rose-colored spots are a sign of typhus."

"Typhus!" one man's voice bellowed. "Now, that's going a bit far, don't you think?"

"How could it be typhus way out here?" another shouted.

As the murmuring slackened, a voice spoke up from the back. "Did you say rose colored spots?" It was Mr. Smith.

"Yes, sir," John nodded.

"We just found a rash on my five-year-old daughter this morning. She's been sick the last couple of days," he replied slowly, his face etched in worry.

"My wife has a rash now, too," another somber voice echoed.

A dreadful silence fell on the group. For a long moment the only sound to be heard was the hooting of some owls in the distance.

"Reverend Garrison," Jacob began. "I think we'd better call a prayer meeting. It seems we need God's help here. I also think we shouldn't plan on moving the wagons tomorrow."

"Does anyone know what causes this?" a voice asked.

Kate spoke up. "The medical book says that rats spread the disease."

John confirmed this.

Lindsey Applegate's voice rose over a murmur of voices. "Gentlemen, we need to send riders to warn the other companies still down in the valley."

"Mr. Applegate?" Kate's female voice stood out about all the men. "The riders need to ask whether anyone has seen any rats."

There were cries of agreement.

"Kate." This time it was Peter Burnett. "Did Dr. Whitman say anything about what we should do if something like this should happen?"

Kate thought for a minute. Then she remembered the Lenox girls' fevers. "He told me once that when fevers hit more than one person, the only thing to do is to isolate the sick people so they won't infect the rest."

"Do you mean a quarantine?" someone asked. "Forced isolation?"

Kate's heart was pounding. She understood the importance of her answer. "Yes," she replied solemnly. "A quarantine."

Kate knew what they were all now thinking. They didn't want to be separated from their loved ones.

But, if they didn't find a way to stop this—and soon—it could wipe out the entire wagon train.

53

RATS

Friday, October 6

On Thursday morning the first snow had fallen, a frightening reminder that winter wasn't far off. Even though this had hampered their efforts to prepare the quarantine area, the emigrants had spent the entire day clearing a site. Then they had erected a number of tents, divided into different groups for men, women, and children. The riders that had been dispatched to all the other companies of wagons had straggled back to the Applegates' wagon through the course of the day. No reports of rats.

Friday morning had dawned cold and overcast, just like the somber mood of the people who now hovered quietly around the snowy edge of the small clearing.

Before breakfast Reverend Garrison had led the company in prayer at the Applegates' wagon. Many of the women had wept openly, pleading with God for the lives of their children. They had all asked for His help to stop the spread of the typhus and heal those who had come down with it.

After breakfast family members had carried their sick loved ones into the quarantine area and left them with the volunteers, but then they gathered around the perimeter in a sort of silent vigil, each wrapped in his or her own thoughts. The forest had become quiet, eerily quiet. Even the dark-eyed juncos had no song for the day.

Though the snow had dampened much of the firewood, Reverend Garrison and Lancefield Johnson had been able to start a fire. A cast-iron kettle hung from a pole over the fire trench, and Jane Mills Vaughn stirred a large pot of warm bean broth. Catherine Stevenson deposited a worn bedroll and a well-used feather pillow on a blanket near the women's tents for anyone who needed them.

The wrinkles in Papa's face had deepened into worry as he handed his ten-year-old son, wrapped in their family quilt, to Ole Joe and stepped back away from the tent. Kate held back the flap so Joe could bend down and carry Jake inside. Joe had volunteered to help with the children, and Kate was helping wherever she was needed. Right now it was here with her brother. Papa didn't say a word. Neither did Joe or Kate.

Kate stepped around the water bucket and ducked inside. In spite of the bitter cold outside, the inside seemed unnaturally warm. Warren Applegate's young face looked ashen against the navy blanket and a frightened Francis Lenox had curled up into a tiny ball in one corner. As Joe settled Jake on another blanket, Kate realized that a tent full of children who weren't talking or playing felt eerie.

Just then Kate heard a familiar voice outside.

"Kate! Are you in there?" it said.

"John, you can't come in here," Kate spoke through the thick canvas. "I've been exposed."

"So have I," he whispered. "I just took Atkins to the men's quarantine. Listen, I want to help you find the source."

"No one has seen any rats, John," Kate replied, shoving the left sleeve of her jacket up to her elbow. "It's got to be something else."

"It *is* rats," John was adamant. "That's what happened in Philly. It was the fleas from infected rats, and the sign was the rash."

"All right then, we'd better ask God to show us what's really going on. He's the only one who knows."

A few hours later Kate returned to their wagon to rest. Papa and Joe were nowhere in sight and neither was Scout. Midnight was munching on some grass, tethered to a nearby tree with Tess right beside him. Caleb bellowed a hello as if to ask her where she had been all morning. The other oxen looked up, probably wondering why they weren't hauling wagons this day. Faithful to the end, with ribs now showing through their skin, they lay close to the trees to which Joe had tied them.

The wagon lurched when she hopped onto it to search around in the back for a blanket. She wasn't sure whether she felt the cold more today because the temperature was dropping or because of the strong sense of foreboding that hovered over her. John was right. They had to find the source of this thing. Soon.

After deciding to sit on a dry spot on the wagon's wooden tongue, her eyes caught sight of her mother's rocking chair sitting next to a fir tree. No one had used the rocker since Mama had passed away. No one had wanted to. It brought back too many memories. Still dusted with snow, its bentwood frame seemed to beckon to her. Kate walked over to it.

The white arms of the chair felt smooth and slippery. With her stocking feet on the seat, Kate folded her long skirt over her legs and used her propped knees as a chin rest. She was tired.

"Mama, I wish you were here to help," she spoke into the stillness. "I don't know what to do." She then shifted her short prayer. "Please show me what to do, Lord. You're the only one who can help us."

A few minutes later the sound of twigs breaking under the snow caught Kate's attention. Just down the hill, a rider had stopped at the Applegates' wagon. Suddenly an energetic Scout scampered up to her, his pink tongue breathing hot vapor into the chilly air. Damp but happy, the dog plopped down at her feet. His black paws were soaked with muddy snow.

"Scout, ole boy, did you follow that rider to all the camps? You're a mess." Kate petted him at the base of his wagging black tail.

After a short time, that same rider approached the Winfields' wagon with his gray gelding walking behind him. Wearing a heavy charcoal wool coat that stopped at his knees, the man had a raspy voice. "I'm looking for Miss Winfield," he stated.

"I'm Miss Winfield." Kate stood up and smoothed out her wrinkled skirt. "What can I do for you?"

"Mr. Applegate asked me to come tell you about the rats, Ma'am."

"The rats?"

"Yes, Ma'am. My wife remembers seeing some rats, but it was way back at Fort Boise. Says they were outside the warehouse."

After she had thanked the man, Kate dropped back into her mother's rocking chair. The chill of the fall air crept through the torn sole of her right boot as she rocked, but it was nothing compared with the chills now running up and down her spine. Could that warehouse be the place? What was in it? Her mind whirred like a spinning wheel. Gunpowder. Farming tools. Bottles of whiskey. Medicine. What else? Kate tried to remember. What would attract rats?

Just then Scout's thumping tail alerted her to the presence of someone else. It was John.

"They told me you were here," he announced, stomping frozen caked mud off his boots. "I've been thinking."

"So have I, John." Standing up, she wrapped the blanket tighter like a shawl. "A man just told me his wife saw rats at Fort Boise. What would attract rats?"

"Food."

"What kind? Papa and I went in that general store. They didn't have any food left."

"Nothing at all?"

"No. He told us he'd already sold out."

"Who did he sell to?"

As if God had ordained that moment, shining rays of light pierced through the clouds and brightened the campsite.

Suddenly Kate understood. She stared at John as her words came slowly and deliberately.

"John, he sold to the people who'd gotten there before us. They were part of our train."

"That's it!" John exclaimed.

"But wait," Kate grabbed the sleeve of his jacket before he turned around. "That can't be right. Jake is sick, and our family didn't buy anything at the store. Where did he get it?"

John ran his fingers through his hair absently. "Did Jake eat with anyone else?"

"I don't know," Kate replied. "But we'd better find out."

54

THE SECRET DISCOVERED

Friday, October 6

Back at the quarantine area, John waited outside the children's tent with Scout, who smelled Jake inside and wagged his tail. Kate found her brother awake, but his eyes were closed and his throat was swollen.

"Jake's doin' better, Miz Kate," Joe announced as he placed a cool rag on Warren's forehead. "Fever's down a bit."

"Jake," Kate called, kneeling beside him. "Jake, can you hear me?"

Jake slowly pried open his eyes and squinted, as if the light was too much.

"Have you eaten at any other wagon than ours since Boise?"

"Why?" he asked drowsily, rubbing one bloodshot eye.

"You're not in trouble, Jake." Kate reassured him with a touch on his arm. "I have to find out what's made everybody sick. Did you eat any trail bread or biscuits with anyone else?"

Jake shook his head no.

"Johnnycakes?"

Again a no.

Kate was puzzled. How could Jake be sick with the same symptoms as the others if he hadn't eaten anything that rats might have infected? Maybe she and John were trailing the wrong fox. Maybe it wasn't food from Boise after all. But what else could it be? There had to be a source.

Then she heard Jake's quavering voice, as soft as a whisper. She leaned down closer to listen. "Kate," he stammered. "I might have eaten some of Mrs. Stevenson's cornbread."

"When were you at Mrs. Stevenson's?"

"When Papa sent me to find the cows."

"Jake, did Warren go with you that day?"

174

Jake nodded his head.

"Did he eat cornbread, too?"

Again a nod.

"That's got to be it! I love you!" she cried out. "Joe, I think we've found the source! Take good care of him. I'll be back."

The canvas tent flap flew back as she rushed outside to find John.

"Let's find Mrs. Stephenson," John replied when he heard.

By early afternoon they still had not been able to locate her. No one knew where she was. Even Mrs. Applegate hadn't seen her since the prayer meeting. The anxiety and worry were mounting inside Kate. Every hour that went by meant that more people might come down with typhus. They checked wagon after wagon and couldn't find Mrs. Stevenson. Where *was* she?

At one point John and Kate slumped on a felled spruce tree down toward the valley. The frozen snow on the tree's needles underscored the urgency of their search. If they didn't find the source of the disease soon, and increasing numbers of sick people prevented the emigrants from moving, winter would trap them here in the mountains. Without fresh supplies, they would never survive.

"John, I'm worried," Kate said, as Scout scuttled after a squirrel who had been burying something in the ground close by. The odor of smoke from the wagons in the valley below reached them. "How are we going to find Mrs. Stevenson?"

"We'll find her, Kate. God will lead us to her—I'm sure of it."

"I wish He'd hurry!"

As John was agreeing, the white forehead of a mustang pushed through a thicket of young pine trees. As the branches parted, Kate recognized the horse of the Indian named Stickus.

"Stickus!" she yelled. "Stickus!"

The Indian reined his horse to a stop and acknowledged them with a nod. Kate turned to John. "Maybe he can help us," she suggested, scrambling to her feet. "I think he's been down in the valley."

Kate silently prayed, "Lord, show me how to communicate with this man."

Slowly Kate pointed first to herself and then at John. How could she make him understand that they needed to find Mrs. Stephenson out of the hundreds of emigrant women?

The idea came into her mind like the breaking of dawn.

Kate pointed to Scout, who was sitting close by watching the mustang. She then raised two fingers. With both palms in the air, Kate tried to look like she had a question.

Stickus realized she was trying to talk to him and looked at her intently.

Did the Indian even understand that she was asking a question? Kate hoped so. She again pointed at Scout, raised two fingers, and shrugged her shoulders.

"Get Scout over here," John suggested.

Kate whistled and amazingly, Scout obeyed. The dog tiptoed over with its tail between its legs, as if he had done something wrong.

"It's all right, boy," she said. "You're not in trouble." Kate bent down and scratched Scout behind the ears. Raising two fingers again, she cocked her head with a question and pointed down into the valley.

All at once, the Indian sat up tall in the saddle and said something. Although she couldn't understand his words, Stickus beckoned them to come with his finger.

Sure enough, within ten minutes he had led them to two dogs with silver heads and black muzzles—the Stevenson's mastiffs. Tied outside Jane Vaughn's wagon, the dogs were waiting for their mistress. Scout wasn't happy to see them, but Kate was ecstatic. They had done it!

And Kate had managed to communicate with an Indian, all on her own.

They found Catherine and Jane busily preparing more soup to take to the people who were sick.

"Mrs. Stevenson," Kate began, almost breathless with excitement. "Did you happen to buy any food supplies at Fort Boise?"

Catherine wiped her hands on her muslin apron, stained from weeks without washing. "I did, Kate," she replied. "But I've never seen any rats."

"Was it cornmeal?"

"It was. I actually bought the last bag."

John went on. "Do you happen to know how much he sold before you, Mrs. Stevenson?"

"No. But I do know that Louesa Lenox bought a bag because we talked about it."

"The clerk told Papa he had quite a bit, John, but sold it all before we got there," Kate interjected.

That was it! Now they knew. The corn meal from Fort Boise had been infected by rats carrying typhus.

She had found the source! With God's help, she had found the source!

Late that afternoon riders thundered through the forest and down the mountain from Captain Applegate's wagon. They had orders to tell everyone that the cornmeal from Fort Boise was infected with typhus, and that all cornmeal obtained there must be buried immediately.

They were also told to announce that the efforts of Miss Kate Winfield had saved the wagon train.

55

"THE BEST POTATOES
I EVER HAD!"

Thursday–Tuesday, October 12–17

On a sunny Thursday October morning, Kate and John were riding through lush grass beside the Umatilla River. Flowing out of the Blue Mountains, the river rippled through a broad, gently rolling valley. Here the emigrants had pitched camp for a few days to rest after their ordeal.

For four days the Company had laid by up in the mountains to tend the sick and give them time to recover. Sadly two more people had died while the disease ran its course, but thankfully, by the end of the fourth day, no one else was getting sick. Although many were still weak, Captain Applegate had issued the order to move out on the eighth of October.

Following Stickus's directions, they had chopped their way up the slopes until they had finally emerged above the tree line. There they had enjoyed their first breathtaking view of the snow-crowned Cascade Mountains to the west. Their descent into the valley had been much easier.

Now the emigrants' wagons were spread across the valley in scattered smaller units, preparing for the last leg of their journey. Some would soon be heading west toward the Columbia River and the Willamette Valley, while those who desperately needed more supplies were following Stickus north up to Dr. Whitman's mission at Walla Walla.

Last night the word had come from Arkansas that there was a Cayuse Indian village just three miles from their campsite, and that the natives were more than willing to trade fresh vegetables for clothing. With Papa's permission, she and John had loaded their horses with vests and shirts—mostly pieces once owned by Douglas Osborne—and had set out this morning on a trading expedition to the village. The prospect of fresh potatoes, corn, and peas was like a dream. She had stopped trying to remember what fresh vegetables tasted like.

But an even stronger draw was Kate's attraction to these strange Native American people, an attraction that had been growing for the entire journey. When she heard that another tribe, the Cayuse, was nearby, Kate knew she couldn't stay away. As a compass needle is drawn to the north, the Indians were pulling on her heart.

Soon she and John were approaching the largest Indian village she had seen yet. Kate flicked Midnight's reins on his neck and urged him forward past fields of corn and peas and potatoes, waiting to be harvested.

The village consisted of dozens of longhouses, constructed by lodge-poles covered with mats of tule leaves. Its occupants were busy—a woman in a plaid skirt was weaving a large blanket held up by poles and rope, while two other women were stirring some kind of liquid in a round stone pit. A young man was patching birch bark canoes that rested on the bank of the river.

A group of Cayuse women wearing freshly tanned animal skins and beaded moccasins greeted them. Kate was suddenly aware of the filthiness of her stained skirt, but the Indian women didn't seem to notice.

The trading was conducted easily, with sign language and smiles on all sides. Kate and John happily returned to camp, their horses loaded with enough fresh vegetables and fish to last them for the rest of their journey to the Whitman mission.

On the ride back to camp, though, Kate kept thinking about the stark contrast between the Cayuse Indians they had just been with and the emaciated tribe of Shoshone back at Salmon Falls. The Cayuse lived with abundance—their soil was good and their crops plentiful. They had warm clothes, and their longhouses were strong and could withstand the winter. The Salmon Falls Shoshone were malnourished and lived in poverty. How could they survive? Couldn't something be done to help them?

After supper that evening Old Joe was thoughtful, his wisdom stick in his lap, and his pipe in his mouth. "Miz Kate, God's hand of mercy's been on us the whole way, 'specially back there in them mountains." Joe gestured behind them with his pipe.

"What do you mean, Joe?" Kate asked, licking the juice from the broiled salmon off her fingertips as she rocked in her Mama's chair.

"Many more folks could've died from the fever." Joe put down his pipe and opened his fiddle case. "And He sure 'nuff showed you what was causin' it."

"You're right there, Joe," Papa chimed in, scraping one last bite of boiled potato off his plate. "And the livestock have come through right well—not many losses."

John scooped up the last of the peas off his tin plate. "God has provided for us the whole way, hasn't He? Look at the food we're eating. We never really ran out of provisions, did we?"

"Nope," said Jake. "But I'm sure glad not to see any beans for awhile." Fully recovered, Jake popped a small potato in his mouth and smacked his lips. "These are the best potatoes I ever had! And, if I don't ever eat another bean, I'll be happy."

Everyone laughed. It was welcome laughter—the kind that comes with knowing that you've come to the end of hard times.

Joe's lighthearted fiddle soon drew a crowd of emigrants, who slowly began once again to dance and laugh as they had done so long ago back on the prairie.

As Kate lay down in the tent, her last waking thoughts were of the half-naked Shoshone children at their village near Salmon Falls.

Sadly the next morning, the time came for Kate to start saying goodbye. Along with scores of others, Jane and William Vaughn were traveling west toward the Columbia River. There they would build rafts and float toward the Pacific. Kate and Jane promised to write each other. Jake gave a bear hug to Arkansas, who was escorting the others as far as the river. Wiping away a tear, Kate thanked the wizened ole mountain man, and told him she would never forget him and all his wonderful stories—stories she would be sure to tell her children someday.

On Monday their little company of tattered wagons finally rolled into the mission. A large two-story adobe house overlooked a pond and a mud-chinked grist mill, where grain was ground into flour. A granary stored fresh grain, and in between it and the house were the blacksmith shop and the corral.

Narcissa Whitman, a large woman with pale skin and auburn hair, had been waiting for them. Under her gingham sunbonnet kind gray eyes smiled a warm greeting. Kate found herself wishing that she had a calico dress that was as clean and starched as Mrs. Whitman's.

For the next two days the men repaired wagons, exchanged exhausted oxen and cows for fresh ones, and purchased such staples as flour and sugar. On the morning of the 17th, it was time to say more farewells. Once again it was hard.

Jake threw fake boxing punches at Warren and Elisha as Mr. Applegate shook Ole Joe's hand. With Kate at his side, Papa spoke to Mrs. Stevenson, telling her he would like to come to call on her again in the Willamette Valley after he arrived. She smiled and said he would be most welcome. While Lancefield Johnson ran the tie strap through the cinch ring of his horse's saddle, Mr. Atkins was directing those within earshot to come and visit him for "the best buffalo meat west of the Mississippi."

Kate had been dreading saying goodbye to John, but to her surprise and delight he said that he had decided not to leave, "at least not yet."

56

"HE HAS CHOSEN YOU"

Wednesday, October 18

On Wednesday afternoon, as the gold and orange of fall splashed the surrounding hills with its splendor, Kate strolled down to the mill pond. Scout scampered on ahead chasing the mallard ducks. Puffy white clouds created imaginary giants and teepees and canoes overhead. Papa and John stood outside the Whitmans' house, discussing something, while nearby Jake was trying to whittle with Papa's knife. She could hear Joe banging against the iron rim of that same front left wagon wheel and knew that Papa would be glad to finally stop traveling and use the wood from the wagon bed as part of their cabin. The hope that Joe would be there "thinkin' on things" warmed her heart.

Independence, Missouri, seemed like a lifetime ago. Though it had only been six months, Kate had lived through much: she had overcome vicious storms, blistering heat, choking alkali dust, and perilous river crossings. She had learned how to cook over a trench fire, how to sew a bull boat, and how to fight deadly diseases.

She had survived the wilderness; she had become a pioneer woman.

She had also suffered through a grievous loss.

Kate's eyes scanned the cornstalks waving with the fall breeze in the field in front of her. *Mama would've liked it here,* she thought. *It's a beautiful place to plant our seeds and start a farm.*

Just then a voice behind her interrupted her thoughts. It was Dr. Whitman. Wearing a clean fresh white linen shirt and black ascot, the doctor held an ancient red leather pouch in one hand.

"May we sit a spell, Kate?" he asked.

Three mallard ducks congregated close by the wooden bench, quacking for some bread crumbs. But Scout soon sent them waddling back down into the pond. A flock of honking geese soared overhead heading south for the winter.

"Kate, I heard about what happened up in the Blues. The typhus must have been horrible."

Kate smiled. "Yes, sir, it was," she replied softly. "But God was with us."

The doctor positioned the leather pouch on his knee. "Before I left you at Farewell Bend, I know you were angry with God because He let your mother die. That's perfectly understandable. All of us get mad at God at some point, because He allows terrible things to happen that make no sense."

Kate wondered where the doctor was headed with this. He continued.

"We know that He loves us—the Bible tells us so. But, when these awful things happen, and we begin to doubt His love for us, then we must choose to trust Him in spite of not understanding. I believe you've made that choice, Kate."

Kate thought for a moment. Had she chosen to trust God, she wondered? "I think I have, Dr. Whitman," Kate responded with some hesitation. "I still don't understand why He let Mama die. But I do know that He loves me—I know He loves us all."

"Indeed He does, Kate. And He has a plan for each of our lives. I think you've been sensing His plan for a long time now."

While it was true that Kate had a dream, she had never really looked on her dream as being God's plan.

Whitman watched more geese fly overhead. "God plants certain desires in our heart—desires we sometimes think are just fantasies. But if we'll follow them, no matter how many obstacles we have to overcome, they turn out to be His plan for us."

Kate perked up. Could the doctor possibly be talking about her dream to become a missionary, and a doctor too? That would be too good to be true. Yet, hadn't Mama told her to let God take care of it?

"Doctor, you know how much I like helping people who are sick," she responded. "Just like Mama did. But I've also found myself drawn to the Indians I've seen."

"Any particular ones?" he asked.

"Yes, my heart really went out to those poor Shoshone back at Salmon Falls. They have nothing. Arkansas told me many of them starve during the winter. I wish I could help them like you and Mrs. Whitman are helping the Cayuse."

"Ah, well, perhaps you can," he mused. "You certainly have learned to care for people, Kate. The people in your company have all spoken of how you saved the wagon train from the typhus epidemic. Every one of them mentioned how determined you were to stop the spread of the disease and find its cause."

Kate was grateful for the compliment, but then she added something. "John helped me, Dr. Whitman. I couldn't have done it without him."

A twinkle shone in the doctor's brown eyes. "God doesn't usually call us to do things alone, Kate—especially when He calls a woman to minister to Indians way out here in the wilderness." He nodded his head in the direction of the house. "I believe God has already provided someone to help you."

He meant John! Was the doctor talking about marriage?

"Everything happens for a reason in God's kingdom, Kate. The hard things He let you experience on the trail forced you to grow up, emotionally and spiritually. You've made good choices and showed that you truly care about other people."

The doctor untied the silk tie around the leather pouch. As he pulled out the cross, it sparkled in the afternoon sun. Worked in fine filigree, it had a red ruby at the end of each arm and another at the cross's center. He handed it to Kate. The silver filigree on the cross was as thin as lace.

"This is the cross I told you about back on the trail. My role is to give this cross to a young person who will commit himself or herself to a life worthy of the One who died upon it to forgive our sins. I believe God is calling you to live such a life among the Indians."

"You mean it doesn't go just to men?" Kate asked, amazed by this sudden change of events. "You could give it to a woman?"

The doctor laughed. "It goes to whomever God chooses, Kate, man or woman. And He has chosen you. I've also spoken with your father about this and with Narcissa. Both of them give their blessing."

Kate could barely believe her ears. Had Papa actually changed his mind about women and doctoring? Had he blessed the idea of her becoming a missionary doctor?

It was a miracle! A God-given miracle.

"It isn't to be worn, however," Whitman went on. "It's much too valuable to risk losing it. Safeguard this treasure with your life, Kate, and carry the meaning of it in your heart until that time when you are older and God shows you the young person to whom you must give it."

As Kate reached out her hand to take the pouch, her eyes filled with tears. She was unable to say a word, stunned by the thought that God would select her, a young woman, as the next person to receive the precious Crimson Cross. She silently prayed that the Savior whose death it symbolized would enable her to be a channel of His love and truth to the Shoshone Indians.

As they hiked back up to the house, Kate cradled the pouch in her hands and took a deep breath of the fresh fall air. Everything felt crisp and clean, as if life was beginning anew.

When the doctor opened the plank door to the house, Kate found everyone inside.

"I'm glad you're back," Mrs. Whitman announced. "We'll have our tea now."

As Mrs. Whitman poured, John spoke up. "Mr. Winfield, with your permission I'd like to take Kate on a walk this afternoon. I have a question I'd like to ask her."

John's dark green shirt brought out the green in his eyes. They were such beautiful eyes.

Kate knew what the question might be.

And amazingly enough, she now knew her answer.

HISTORICAL NOTE

More than three hundred thousand Americans went up the Oregon Trail to Oregon or California. It was the greatest human migration in world history. Hollywood movies used to depict Indian attacks as the most dangerous part of the journey, but prior to 1860, the greatest danger on the Oregon Trail was actually fatal diseases, particularly typhus and cholera. There was no typhus epidemic on the 1843 wagon train, but we made this the climax of our story because epidemics were common on later wagon trains.

Kate and her family are fictional characters, but her experiences reflect actual events on the 1843 wagon train. Every physical location in the story can be found with the help of guidebooks and maps, although none of the actual forts still exist.

We researched emigrant diaries from the 1843 wagon train and collated eight of them to create an accurate timetable of the journey. This was not easy, because different parts of the wagon train arrived at places at different times. We deliberately changed only one date: In our story Jane Mills climbs Independence Rock with Kate on July 27, whereas in truth her name was carved there by James Nesmith on July 30.

Dr. Marcus Whitman, his wife Narcissa, and Henry and Eliza Spaulding were the first American missionaries to the Indians of the Pacific Northwest. In 1836 they blazed the trail for future emigrant wagon trains by trekking overland from the East, arriving in the Oregon Territory with a two-wheel wagon.

Why did we choose the 1843 Oregon Emigrating Company's wagon train for our story? We wanted Dr. Whitman to be the one to give Kate the Crimson Cross, and when we found that he returned home from a trip back East on that train, it was obvious that the 1843 wagon train was the one for our story!

We invented John Prentiss and his three companions from the East, but Oregon Trail diaries often mention "greenhorn" type Easterners and the fatal accidents they had with guns. Tragically it was also common for children to be run over by the wagon wheels.

The fabled mountain men and fur trappers occupy a special place in the lore of the American West. When the fur trade played out, they often became guides for wagon trains on the Oregon Trail. Arkansas is a fictional character, but he is typical of that storied breed of men.

The Applegates, the Stevensons, the Lenoxes, the Burnetts, Joel Hembree, and Stickus—all were real persons on the 1843 wagon train. Old Man Eyers did drown in the Snake River.

There was no Preacher Garrison with them, but he is typical of the dedicated Methodist circuit riders of the time.

One of the boys on the 1843 wagon train *did* get his head caught in a dead ox's stomach, exactly as we depicted it! His name was Andy Baker, but it was certainly the kind of thing that Jake would do, so we couldn't resist.

We hope that you enjoyed reading this story of the Oregon Trail as much as we did writing it.

Enjoy the other
3 books in the
CRIMSON CROSS
juvenile fiction series!

Mercy Clifton: Pilgrim Girl
$9.99
ISBN: 978-0-8054-4395-0

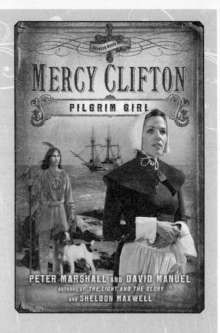

Nate Donovan: Revolutionary
Spy $9.99
ISBN: 978-0-8054-4394-3

Pedro de Torreros and
the Voyage of Destiny
$9.99
ISBN: 978-0-8054-4396-7

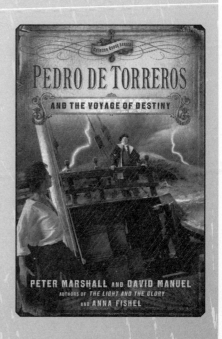

The Crimson Cross books are
written by best-selling authors
Peter Marshall and David Manuel
(*The Light and the Glory* and *From
Sea to Shining Sea*).